One Day's Courtship
and
The Heralds of Fame

ROBERT BARR

1st WORLD
LIBRARY
Literary Society

One Day's Courtship

Robert Barr

© 1st World Library – Literary Society, 2004
PO Box 2211
Fairfield, IA 52556
www.1stworldlibrary.org
First Edition

LCCN: 2004195347

Softcover ISBN: 1-4218-0181-7
Hardcover ISBN: 1-4218-0081-0
eBook ISBN: 1-4218-0281-3

Purchase *"One Day's Courtship"*
as a traditional bound book at:
www.1stWorldLibrary.org/purchase.asp?ISBN=1-4218-0181-7

One Day's Courtship
contributed by Tim, Ed & Rodney
in support of
1st World Library Literary Society

ONE DAY'S COURTSHIP

CHAPTER I.

John Trenton, artist, put the finishing touches to the letter he was writing, and then read it over to himself. It ran as follows: -

"MY DEAR ED.,

"I sail for England on the 27th. But before I leave I want to have another look at the Shawenegan Falls. Their roar has been in my ears ever since I left there. That tremendous hillside of foam is before my eyes night and day. The sketches I took are not at all satisfactory, so this time I will bring my camera with me, and try to get some snapshots at the falls.

"Now, what I ask is this. I want you to hold that canoe for me against all comers for Tuesday. Also, those two expert half-breeds. Tell them I am coming, and that there is money in it if they take me up and back as safely as they did before. I don't suppose there will be much demand for the canoe on that day; in fact, it astonishes me that Americans, who appreciate the good things of our country better than we do ourselves, practically know nothing of this superb cataract right at their own doors. I suppose your new canoe is not finished yet, and as the others are up in the woods I write so that you will keep this particular craft for me. I do not wish to take any risks, as I leave so soon. Please drop me a note to this hotel at Quebec, and I will meet you in Le Gres on Tuesday morning at daybreak.

"Your friend,

"JOHN TRENTON."

Mason was a millionaire and a lumber king, but every one called him Ed. He owned baronial estates in the pine woods, and saw-mills without number. Trenton had brought a letter of introduction to him from a mutual friend in Quebec, who had urged the artist to visit the Shawenegan Falls. He heard the Englishman inquire about the cataract, and told him that he knew the man who would give him every facility for reaching the falls. Trenton's acquaintance with Mason was about a fortnight old, but already they were the firmest of friends. Any one who appreciated the Shawenegan Falls found a ready path to the heart of the big lumberman. It was almost impossible to reach the falls without the assistance of Mr. Mason. However, he was no monopolist. Any person wishing to visit the cataract got a canoe from the lumber king free of all cost, except a tip to the two boatmen who acted as guides and watermen. The artist had not long to wait for his answer. It was -

"My DEAR JOHN,

"The canoe is yours; the boatmen are yours: and the Shawenegan is yours for Tuesday. Also,

Robert Barr

"I am yours,

"E. MASON."

On Monday evening John Trenton stepped off the C.P.R. train at Three Rivers. With a roughing-it suit on, and his camera slung over his shoulders, no one would have taken him for the successful landscape artist who on Piccadilly was somewhat particular about his attire.

John Trenton was not yet R.A., nor even A.R.A., but all his friends would tell you that, if the Royal Academy was not governed by a clique, he would have been admitted long ago, and that anyhow it was only a question of time. In fact, John admitted this to himself, but to no one else.

He entered the ramshackle 'bus, and was driven a long distance through very sandy streets to the hotel on the St. Lawrence, and, securing a room, made arrangements to be called before daybreak. He engaged the same driver who had taken him out to "The Greys," as it was, locally called, on the occasion of his-former visit.

The morning was cold and dark. Trenton found the buckboard at the door, and he put his camera under the one seat - a kind of a box for the holding of bits of harness and other odds and ends. As he buttoned up his overcoat he noticed that a great white steamer had come in the night, and was tied up in front of the hotel.

"The Montreal boat," explained the driver.

As they drove along the silent streets of Three Rivers,

Trenton called to mind how, on the former occasion, he thought the Lower Canada buckboard by all odds, the most uncomfortable vehicle he had ever ridden in, and he felt that his present experience was going to corroborate this first impression. The seat was set in the centre, between the front and back wheels, on springy boards, and every time the conveyance jolted over a log - a not unfrequent occurrence - the seat went down and the back bent forward, as if to throw him over on the heels of the patient horse.

The road at first was long and straight and sandy, but during the latter part of the ride there were plenty of hills, up many of which a plank roadway ran; so that loads which it would be impossible to take through the deep sand, might be hauled up the steep incline.

At first the houses they passed had a dark and deserted look; then a light twinkled here and there. The early habitant was making his fire. As daylight began gradually to bring out the landscape, the sharp sound of the distant axe was heard. The early habitant was laying in his day's supply of firewood.

"Do you notice how the dawn slowly materialises the landscape?" said the artist to the boy beside him.

The boy saw nothing wonderful about that. Daylight always did it.

"Then it is not unusual in these parts? You see, I am very seldom up at this hour."

The boy wished that was his case.

"Does it not remind you of a photographer in a dark

room carefully developing a landscape plate? Not one of those rapid plates, you know, but a slow, deliberate plate."

No, it didn't remind him of anything of the kind. He had never seen either a slow or a rapid plate developed.

"Then you have no prejudices as to which is the best developer, pyrogallic acid or ferrous oxalate, not to mention such recent decoctions as eikonogen, quinol, and other?"

No, the boy had none.

"Well, that's what I like. I like a young man whose mind is open to conviction."

The boy was not a conversational success. He evidently did not enter into the spirit of the artist's remarks. He said most people got off at that point and walked to warm up, and asked Trenton if he would not like to follow their example.

"No, my boy," said the Englishman, "I don't think I shall. You see, I have paid for this ride, and I want to get all I can out of it. I shall shiver here and try to get the worth of my money. But with you it is different. If you want to get down, do so. I will drive."

The boy willingly handed over the reins, and sprang out on the road. Trenton, who was a boy himself that morning, at once whipped up the horse and dashed down the hill to get away from the driver. When a good half-mile had been worried out of the astonished animal, Trenton looked back to see the driver come panting after. The young man was calmly sitting on the back part of the buckboard, and when the horse began to walk again, the boy slid off, and, without a smile on his face, trotted along at the side.

"That fellow has evidently a quiet sense of humour, although he is so careful not to show it," said Trenton to himself.

On reaching the hilltop, they caught a glimpse of the rim of the sun rising gloriously over the treetops on the other side of the St. Maurice River. Trenton stopped the horse, and the boy looked up to see what was wrong. He could not imagine any one stopping merely to look at the sun.

"Isn't that splendid?" cried Trenton, with a deep breath, as he watched the great globe slowly ascend into the sky. The distant branches of the trees were delicately etched against its glowing surface, and seemed to cling to it like tendrils, slipping further and further down as the sun leisurely disentangled itself, and at last stood in its incomparable grandeur full above the forest.

The woods all around had on their marvellous autumn tints, and now the sun added a living lustre to them that made the landscape more brilliant than anything the artist had ever seen before.

"Ye gods!" he cried enthusiastically, "that scene is worth coming from England to have one glimpse of."

"See here," said the driver, "if you want to catch Ed. Mason before he's gone to the woods you'll have to hurry up. It's getting late."

"True, O driver. You have brought me from the sun to

the earth. Have you ever heard of the person who fell from the sun to the earth?"

No, he hadn't.

"Well, that was before your time. You will never take such a tumble. I - I suppose they don't worship the sun in these parts?"

No, they didn't.

"When you come to think of it, that is very strange. Have you ever reflected that it is always in warm countries they worship the sun? Now, I should think ought to be just the other way about. Do you know that when I got on with you this morning I was eighty years old, every day of it. What do you think my age is now?"

"Eighty years, sir."

"Not a bit of it. I'm eighteen. The sun did it. And yet they claim there is no fountain of youth. What fools people are, my boy!"

The young man looked at his fare slyly, and cordially agreed with him.

"You certainly *have* a concealed sense of humour," said the artist.

They wound down a deep cut in the hill, and got a view of the lumber village - their destination. The roar of the waters tumbling over the granite rocks - the rocks from which the village takes its name - came up the ravine. The broad river swept in a great semicircle to their right, and its dark waters were flecked with the foam of the small falls near the village, and the great cataract miles up the river. It promised to be a perfect autumn day. The sky, which had seemed to Trenton overcast when they started, was now one deep dome of blue without even the suggestion of a cloud.

The buckboard drew up at the gate of the house in which Mr. Mason lived when he was in the lumber village, although his home was at Three Rivers. The old Frenchwoman, Mason's housekeeper, opened the door for Trenton, and he remembered as he went in how the exquisite cleanliness of everything had impressed him during his former visit. She smiled as she recognised the genial Englishman. She had not forgotten his compliments in her own language on her housekeeping some months before, and perhaps she also remembered his liberality. Mr. Mason, she said, had gone to the river to see after the canoe, leaving word that he would return in a few minutes. Trenton, who knew the house, opened the door at his right, to enter the sitting-room and leave there his morning wraps, which the increasing warmth rendered no longer necessary. As he burst into the room in his impetuous way, he was taken aback to see standing at the window, looking out towards the river, a tall young woman. Without changing her position, she looked slowly around at the intruder. Trenton's first thought was a hasty wish that he were better dressed. His roughing-it costume, which up to that time had seemed so comfortable, now appeared uncouth and out of place. He felt as if he had suddenly found himself in a London drawing-room with a shooting-jacket on. But this sensation was quickly effaced by the look which the beauty gave him over her shoulder. Trenton, in all his experience, had never encountered such a glance of

Robert Barr

indignant scorn. It was a look of resentment and contempt, with just a dash of feminine reproach in it.

"What have I done?" thought the unhappy man; then he stammered aloud, "I - I - really - I beg your pardon. I thought the - ah - room was empty."

The imperious young woman made no reply. She turned to the window again, and Trenton backed out of the room as best he could.

"Well!" he said to himself, as he breathed with relief the outside air again, "that was the rudest thing I ever knew a lady to do. She *is* a lady, there is no doubt of that. There is nothing of the backwoods about her. But she might at least have answered me. What have I done, I wonder? It must be something terrible and utterly unforgivable, whatever it is. Great heavens!" he murmured, aghast at the thought, "I hope that girl isn't going up to the Shawenegan Falls."

Trenton was no ladies' man. The presence of women always disconcerted him, and made him feel awkward and boorish. He had been too much of a student in higher art to acquire the smaller art of the drawing-room. He felt ill at ease in society, and seemed to have a fatal predilection for saying the wrong thing, and suffered the torture afterwards of remembering what the right thing would have been.

Trenton stood at the gate for a moment, hoping Mason would come. Suddenly he remembered with confusion that he was directly in range of those disdainful eyes in the parlour, and he beat a hasty retreat toward the old mill that stood by the falls. The roar of the turbulent water over the granite rocks had a soothing effect on the soul of the man who knew he was a criminal, yet could not for the life of him tell what his crime had been. Then he wandered up the river-bank toward where he saw the two half-breeds placing the canoe in the still water at the further end of the village. Half-way there he was relieved to meet the genial Ed. Mason, who greeted him, as Trenton thought, with a somewhat overwrought effusion. There evidently was something on the genial Ed.'s mind.

"Hello, old man," he cried, shaking Trenton warmly by the hand. "Been here long? Well, I declare, I'm glad to see you. Going to have a splendid day for it, aren't you? Yes, sir, I *am* glad to see you."

"When a man says that twice in one breath, a fellow begins to doubt him. Now, you good-natured humbug, what's the matter? What have I done? How did you find me out? Who turned Queen's evidence? Look here, Edward Mason, why are you *not* glad to see me?"

"Nonsense; you know I am. No one could be more welcome. By the way, my wife's here. You never met her, I think?"

"I saw a young lady remarkably -"

"No, no; that is Miss - By the way, Trenton, I want you to do me a favour, now that I think of it. Of course the canoe is yours for to-day, but that young woman wants to go up to the Shawenegan. You wouldn't mind her going up with you, would you? You see, I have no other canoe to-day, and she can't stay till to-morrow."

"I shall be delighted, I'm sure," answered Trenton. But he didn't look it.

CHAPTER II.

Eva Sommerton, of Boston, knew that she lived in the right portion of that justly celebrated city, and this knowledge was evident in the poise of her queenly head, and in every movement of her graceful form. Blundering foreigners - foreigners as far as Boston is concerned, although they may be citizens of the United States - considered Boston to be a large city, with commerce and railroads and busy streets and enterprising newspapers, but the true Bostonian knows that this view is very incorrect. The real Boston is penetrated by no railroads. Even the jingle of the street-car bell does not disturb the silence of the streets of this select city. It is to the ordinary Boston what the empty, out-of-season London is to the rest of the busy metropolis. The stranger, jostled by the throng, may not notice that London is empty, but his lordship, if he happens during the deserted period to pass through, knows there is not a soul in town.

Miss Sommerton had many delusions, but fortunately for her peace of mind she had never yet met a candid friend with courage enough to tell her so. It would have required more bravery than the ordinary society person possesses to tell Miss Sommerton about any of her faults. The young gentlemen of her acquaintance claimed that she had no faults, and if her lady friends thought otherwise, they reserved the expression of such opinions for social gatherings not graced by the presence of Miss Sommerton.

Eva Sommerton thought she was not proud, or if there was any tinge of pride in her character, it was pride of the necessary and proper sort.

She also possessed the vain belief that true merit was the one essential, but if true merit had had the misfortune to be presented to Miss Sommerton without an introduction of a strictly unimpeachable nature, there is every reason to fear true merit would not have had the exquisite privilege of basking in the smiles of that young Bostonian. But perhaps her chief delusion was the belief that she was an artist. She had learned all that Boston could teach of drawing, and this thin veneer had received a beautiful foreign polish abroad. Her friends pronounced her sketches really wonderful. Perhaps if Miss Sommerton's entire capital had been something less than her half-yearly income, she might have made a name for herself; but the rich man gets a foretaste of the scriptural difficulty awaiting him at the gates of heaven, when he endeavours to achieve an earthly success, the price of which is hard labour, and not hard cash.

We are told that pride must have a fall, and there came an episode in Miss Sommerton's career as an artist which was a rude shock to her self-complacency. Having purchased a landscape by a celebrated artist whose work she had long admired, she at last ventured to write to him and enclose some of her own sketches, with a request for a candid judgment of them - that is, she *said* she wanted a candid judgment of them.

The reply seemed to her so ungentlemanly, and so

Robert Barr

harsh, that, in her vexation and anger, she tore the letter to shreds and stamped her pretty foot with a vehemence which would have shocked those who knew her only as the dignified and self-possessed Miss Eva Sommerton.

Then she looked at her libelled sketches, and somehow they did not appear to be quite so faultless as she had supposed them to be.

This inspection was followed by a thoughtful and tearful period of meditation; and finally, with contriteness, the young woman picked up from her studio floor the shreds of the letter and pasted them carefully together on a white sheet of paper, in which form she still preserved the first honest opinion she had ever received.

In the seclusion of her aesthetic studio Miss Sommerton made a heroic resolve to work hard. Her life was to be consecrated to art. She would win reluctant recognition from the masters. Under all this wave of heroic resolution was an under-current of determination to get even with the artist who had treated her work so contemptuously.

Few of us quite live up to our best intentions, and Miss Sommerton was no exception to the rule. She did not work as devotedly as she had hoped to do, nor did she become a recluse from society. A year after she sent to the artist some sketches which she had taken in Quebec - some unknown waterfalls, some wild river scenery - and received from him a warmer letter of commendation than she had hoped for. He remembered her former sketches, and now saw a great improvement. If the waterfall sketches were not exaggerations, he would like to see the originals. Where were they? The lady was proud of her discoveries in the almost unknown land of Northern Quebec, and she wrote a long letter telling all about them, and a polite note of thanks for the information ended the correspondence.

Miss Sommerton's favourite discovery was that tremendous downward plunge of the St. Maurice, the Falls of Shawenegan. She had sketched it from a dozen different standpoints, and raved about it to her friends, if such a dignified young person as Miss Sommerton could be said to rave over anything. Some Boston people, on her recommendation, had visited the falls, but their account of the journey made so much of the difficulties and discomforts, and so little of the magnificence of the cataract, that our amateur artist resolved to keep the falls, as it were, to herself. She made yearly pilgrimages to the St. Maurice, and came to have a kind of idea of possession which always amused Mr. Mason. She seemed to resent the fact that others went to look at the falls, and, worse than all, took picnic baskets there, actually lunching on its sacred shores, leaving empty champagne bottles and boxes of sardines that had evidently broken some one's favourite knife in the opening. This particular summer she had driven out to "The Greys," but finding that a party was going up in canoes every day that week, she promptly ordered her driver to take her back to Three Rivers, saying to Mr. Mason she would return when she could have the falls to herself."

"You remind me of Miss Porter," said the lumber king.

"Miss Porter! Who is she?"

"When Miss Porter visited England and saw Mr.

Gladstone, he asked her if she had ever seen the Niagara Falls. 'Seen them?' she answered. 'Why, I *own* them!'"

"What did she mean by that? I confess I don't see the point, or perhaps it isn't a joke."

"Oh yes, it is. You mustn't slight my good stories in that way. She meant just what she said. I believe the Porter family own, or did own, Goat Island, and, I suppose, the other bank, and, therefore, the American Fall. The joke - I do dislike to have to explain jokes, especially to you cool, unsympathising Bostonians - is the ridiculousness of any mere human person claiming to own such a thing as the Niagara Falls. I believe, though, that you are quite equal to it - I do indeed."

"Thank you, Mr. Mason."

"I knew you would be grateful when I made myself clearly understood. Now, what I was going to propose is this. You should apply to the Canadian Government for possession of the Shawenegan. I think they would let it go at a reasonable figure. They look on it merely as an annoying impediment to the navigation of the river, and an obstruction which has caused them to spend some thousands of dollars in building a slide by the side of it, so that the logs may come down safely."

"If I owned it, the slide is the first thing I would destroy."

"What? And ruin the lumber industry of the Upper St. Maurice? Oh, you wouldn't do such a thing! If that is your idea, I give you fair warning that I will oppose your claims with all the arts of the lobbyist. If you want to become the private owner of the falls, you should tell the Government that you have some thoughts of encouraging the industries of the province by building a mill -"

"A mill?"

"Yes; why not? Indeed, I have half a notion to put a saw-mill there myself. It always grieves me to see so much magnificent power going to waste."

"Oh, seriously, Mr. Mason, you would never think of committing such an act of sacrilege?"

"Sacrilege, indeed! I like that. Why, the man who makes one saw-mill hum where no mill ever hummed before is a benefactor to his species. Don't they teach political economy at Boston? I thought you liked saw-mills. You drew a very pretty picture of the one down the stream."

"I admire a *ruined* saw-mill, as that one was; but not one in a state of activity, or of eruption, as a person might say."

"Well, won't you go up to the falls to-day, Miss Sommerton? I assure you we have a most unexceptionable party. Why, one of them is a Government official. Think of that!"

"I refuse to think of it; or, if I do think of it, I refuse to be dazzled by his magnificence. I want to see the Shawenegan, not a picnic party drinking.

"You wrong them, really you do, Miss Sommerton, believe me. You have got your dates mixed. It is the champagne party that goes to-day. The beer crowd is not due until to-morrow."

"The principle is the same."

"The price of the refreshment is not. I speak as a man of bitter experience. Let's see. If recollection holds her throne, I think there was a young lady from New England - I forget the name of the town at the moment - who took a lunch with her the last time she went to the Shawenegan. I merely give this as my impression, you know. I am open to contradiction."

"Certainly, I took a lunch. I always do. I would to-day if I were going up there, and Mrs. Mason would give me some sandwiches. You would give me a lunch, wouldn't you, dear?"

"I'll tell them to get it ready now, if you will only stay," replied that lady, on being appealed to.

"No, it isn't the lunch I object to. I object to people going there merely *for* the lunch. I go for the scenery; the lunch is incidental."

"When you get the deed of the falls, I'll tell you what we'll do," put in Mason. "We will have a band of trained Indians stationed at the landing, and they will allow no one to disembark who does not express himself in sufficiently ecstatic terms about the great cataract. You will draw up a set of adjectives, which I will give to the Indians, instructing them to allow no one to land who does not use at least three out of five of them in referring to the falls. People whose eloquent appreciation does not reach the required altitude will have to stay there till it does, that's all. We will treat them as we do our juries - starve them into a verdict, and the right verdict at that."

"Don't mind him, Eva. He is just trying to exasperate you. Think of what I have to put up with. He goes on like that all the time," said Mrs. Mason.

"Really, my dear, your flattery confuses me. You can't persuade any one that I keep up this brilliancy in the privacy of my own house. It is only turned on for company."

"Why, Mr. Mason, I didn't think you looked on me as company. I thought I enjoyed the friendship of the Mason family."

"Oh, you do, you do indeed! The company I referred to was the official party which has just gone to the falls. This is some of the brilliancy left over. But, really, you had better stay after coming all this distance."

"Yes, do, Eva. Let me go back with you to the Three Rivers, and then you stay with me till next week, when you can visit the falls all alone. It is very pleasant at Three Rivers just now. And besides, we can go for a day's shopping at Montreal."

"I wish I could."

"Why, of course you can," said Mason. Imagine the delight of smuggling your purchases back to Boston. Confess that this is a pleasure you hadn't thought of."

"I admit the fascination of it all, but you see I am with a party that has gone on to Quebec, and I just got away for a day. I am to meet them there to-night or to-morrow morning. But I will return in the autumn, Mrs. Mason, when it is too late for the picnics. Then, Mr. Mason, take warning. I mean to have a canoe to myself, or - well, you know the way we Bostonians treated you Britishers once upon a time."

"Distinctly. But we will return good for evil, and give you warm tea instead of the cold mixture you so foolishly brewed in the harbour."

As the buckboard disappeared around the corner, and Mr. and Mrs. Mason walked back to the house, the lady said -

"What a strange girl Eva is."

"Very. Don't she strike you as being a trifle selfish?"

"Selfish? Eva Sommerton? Why, what could make you think such a thing? What an absurd idea! You cannot imagine how kind she was to me when I visited Boston."

"Who could help it, my dear? I would have been so myself if I had happened to meet you there."

"Now, Ed., don't be absurd."

"There is something absurd in being kind to a person's wife, isn't there? Well, it struck me her objection to any one else being at the falls, when her ladyship was there, might seem - not to me, of course, but to an outsider - a trifle selfish."

"Oh, you don't understand her at all. She has an artistic temperament, and she is quite right in wishing to be alone. Now, Ed., when she does come again I want you to keep anyone else from going up there. Don't forget it, as you do most of the things I tell you. Say to anybody who wants to go up that the canoes are out of repair."

"Oh, I can't say that, you know. Anything this side of a crime I am willing to commit; but to perjure myself, no, not for Venice. Can you think of any other method that will combine duplicity with a clear conscience? I'll tell you what I'll do. I will have the canoe drawn up, and gently, but firmly, slit it with my knife. One of the men can mend it in ten minutes. Then I can look even the official from Quebec in the face, and tell him truly that the canoe will not hold water. I suppose as long as my story will hold water you and Miss Sommerton will not mind?"

"If the canoe is ready for her when she comes, I shall be satisfied. Please to remember I am going to spend a week or two in Boston next winter."

"Oh ho, that's it, is it? Then it was not pure philanthropy -"

"Pure nonsense, Ed. I want the canoe to be ready, that's all."

When Mrs. Mason received the letter from Miss Sommerton, stating the time the young woman intended to pay her visit to the Shawenegan, she gave the letter to her husband, and reminded him of the necessity of keeping the canoe for that particular date. As the particular date was some weeks off, and as Ed. Mason was a man who never crossed a stream until he came to it, he said, "All right," put the letter in his inside pocket, and the next time he thought of it was on the fine autumn afternoon - Monday afternoon - when he saw Mrs. Mason drive up to the door of his lumber-woods residence with Miss Eva Sommerton in the buggy beside her. The young lady wondered, as Mr. Mason helped her out, if that genial gentleman, whom she regarded as the most fortunate of men, had in reality some secret, gnawing sorrow the world knew not of.

"Why, Ed., you look ill," exclaimed Mrs. Mason; "is there anything the matter?"

"Oh, it is nothing - at least, not of much consequence. A little business worry, that's all."

"Has there been any trouble?"

"Oh no - at the least, not *yet*."

"Trouble about the men, is it?"

"No, not about the men," said the unfortunate gentle-man, with a somewhat unnecessary emphasis on the last word.

"Oh, Mr. Mason, I am afraid I have come at a wrong time. If so, don't hesitate to tell me. If I can do anything to help you, I hope I may be allowed."

"You have come just at the right time," said the lumberman, "and you are very welcome, I assure you. If I find I need help, as perhaps I may, you will be reminded of your promise."

To put off as long as possible the evil time of meeting

his wife, Mason went with the man to see the horse put away, and he lingered an unnecessarily long time in ascertaining that everything was right in the stable. The man was astonished to find his master so particular that afternoon. A crisis may be postponed, but it can rarely be avoided altogether, and knowing he had to face the inevitable sooner or later, the unhappy man, with a sigh, betook himself to the house, where he found his wife impatiently waiting for him. She closed the door and confronted him.

"Now, Ed., what's the matter?"

"Where's Miss Sommerton?" was the somewhat irrelevant reply.

"She has gone to her room. Ed, don't keep me in suspense. What is wrong?"

"You remember John Trenton, who was here in the summer?"

"I remember hearing you speak of him. I didn't meet him, you know."

"Oh, that's so. Neither you did. You see, he's an awful good fellow, Trenton is - that is, for an Englishman."

"Well, what has Trenton to do with the trouble?"

"Everything, my dear - everything."

"I see how it is. Trenton visited the Shawenegan?"

"He did."

"And he wants to go there again?"

"He does."

"And you have gone and promised him the canoe for to morrow?"

"The intuition of woman, my dear, is the most wonderful thing on earth."

"It is not half so wonderful as the negligence-of man - I won't say the stupidity."

"Thank you, Jennie, for not saying it, but I really think I would feel better if you did."

"Now, what are you going to do about it?"

"Well, my dear, strange as it may appear, that very question has been racking my brain for the last ten minutes. Now, what would you do in my position?"

"Oh, I couldn't be in your position."

"No, that's so, Jennie. Excuse me for suggesting the possibility. I really think this trouble has affected my mind a little. But if you had a husband - if a sensible woman like you *could* have a husband who got himself into such a position - what would you advise him to do?"

"Now, Ed., don't joke. It's too serious."

"My dear, no one on earth can have such a realisation of its seriousness as I have at this moment. I feel as Mark Twain did with that novel he never finished. I have brought things to a point where I can't go any further. The game seems blocked. I wonder if Miss Sommerton would accept ten thousand feet of lumber f.o.b. and call it square."

"Really, Ed., if you can't talk sensibly, I have nothing further to say."

"Well, as I said, the strain is getting too much for me. Now, don't go away, Jennie. Here is what I am thinking of doing. I'll speak to Trenton. He won't mind Miss Sommerton's going in the canoe with him. In fact, I should think he would rather like it."

"Dear me, Ed., is that all the progress you've made? I am not troubling myself about Mr. Trenton. The difficulty will be with Eva. Do you think for a moment she will go if she imagined herself under obligations to a stranger for the canoe? Can't you get Mr. Trenton to put off his visit until the day after tomorrow? It isn't long to wait."

"No, that is impossible. You see, he has just time to catch his steamer as it is. No, he has the promise in writing, while Miss Sommerton has no legal evidence if this thing ever gets into the courts. Trenton has my written promise. You see, I did not remember the two dates were the same. When I wrote to Trenton -"

"Ed., don't try to excuse yourself. You had her letter in your pocket, you know you had. This is a matter for which there is no excuse, and it cannot be explained away."

"That's so, Jennie. I am down in the depths once more. I shall not try to crawl out again - at least, not while my wife is looking."

"No, your plan will not work. I don't know that any will. There is only one thing to try, and it is this - Miss Sommerton must think that the canoe is hers. You must appeal to her generosity to let Mr. Trenton go with her."

"Won't you make the appeal, Jen?"

"No, I will not. In the first place she'll be sorry for you, because you will make such a bungle of it. Trial is your only hope."

"Oh, if success lies in bungling, I will succeed."

"Don't be too sure. I suppose that man will be here by daybreak to-morrow?"

"Not so bad as that, Jennie. You always try to put the worst face on things. He won't be here till sunrise at the earliest."

"I will ask Eva to come down."

"You needn't hurry just because of me. Besides, I would like a few moments to prepare myself for my fate. Even a murderer is given a little time."

"Not a moment, Ed. We had better get this thing settled as soon as possible."

"Perhaps you are right," he murmured, with a deep sigh. "Well, if we Britishers, as Miss S. calls us, ever faced the Americans with as faint a heart as I do now, I don't wonder we got licked."

"Don't say 'licked,' Ed."

"I believe it's historical. Oh, I see. You object to the word, not to the allegation. Well, I won't cavil about that. All my sympathy just now is concentrated on one unfortunate Britisher. My dear, let the sacrifice begin."

Mrs. Mason went to the stairway and called -

"Eva, dear, can you come down for a moment? We want you to help us out of a difficulty."

Miss Sommerton appeared smilingly, smoothing down the front of the dress that had taken the place of the one she travelled in. She advanced towards Mason with sweet compassion in her eyes, and that ill-fated man thought he had never seen any one look so altogether charming - excepting, of course, his own wife in her youthful days. She seemed to have smoothed away all the Boston stiffness as she smoothed her dress.

"Oh, Mr. Mason," she said, sympathetically, as she approached, "I am so sorry anything has happened to trouble you, and I do hope I am not intruding."

"Indeed, you are not, Miss Eva. In fact, your sympathy has taken away half the trouble already, and I want to beg of you to help me off with the other half."

A glance at his wife's face showed him that he had not made a bad beginning.

"Miss Sommerton, you said you would like to kelp me. Now I am going to appeal to you. I throw myself on your mercy."

There was a slight frown on Mrs. Mason's face, and her husband felt that he was perhaps appealing too much.

"In fact, the truth is, my wife gave me -"

Here a cough interrupted him, and he paused and ran his hand through his hair. "Pray don't mind me, Mr. Mason," said Miss Sommerton, "if you would rather not tell -"

"Oh, but I must; that is, I want you to know."

He glanced at his wife, but there was no help there, so he plunged in headlong.

"To tell the truth, there is a friend of mine who wants to go to the falls tomorrow. He sails for Europe immediately, and has no other day."

The Boston rigidity perceptibly returned.

"Oh, if that is all, you needn't have had a moment's trouble. I can just as well put off my visit."

"Oh, can you?" cried Mason, joyously.

His wife sat down in the rocking-chair with a sigh of despair. Her infatuated husband thought he was getting along famously.

"Then your friends are not waiting for you at Quebec this time, and you can stay a day or two with us."

"Eva's friends are at Montreal, Edward, and she cannot stay."

"Oh, then - why, then, to-morrow's *your* only day, too?"

"It doesn't matter in the least, Mr. Mason. I shall be most glad to put off my visit to oblige your friend - no, I didn't mean that," she cried, seeing the look of anguish on Mason's face, "it is to oblige you. Now, am I not good?"

"No, you are cruel," replied Mason. "You are going up to the falls. I insist on that. Let's take that as settled. The canoe is yours." He caught an encouraging look from his wife. "If you want to torture me you will say you will not go. If you want to do me the greatest of favours, you will let my friend go in the canoe with you to the landing."

"What! go alone with a stranger?" cried Miss Sommerton, freezingly.

"No, the Indians will be there, you know."

"Oh, I didn't expect to paddle the canoe myself."

"I don't know about that. You strike me as a girl who would paddle her own canoe pretty well."

"Now, Edward," said his wife. "He wants to take some photographs of the falls, and -"

"Photographs? Why, Ed., I thought you said he was an artist."

"Isn't a photographer an artist?"

"You know he isn't."

"Well, my dear, you know they put on their signs, 'artist - photographer, pictures taken in cloudy weather.' But he's an amateur photographer; an amateur is not so bad as a professional, is he, Miss Sommerton?"

"I think he's worse, if there is any choice. A professional at least takes good pictures, such as they are."

"He is an elderly gentleman, and I am sure -"

"Oh, is he?" cried Miss Sommerton; "then the matter is settled. He shall go. I thought it was some young fop of an amateur photographer."

"Oh, quite elderly. His hair is grey, or badly tinged at least."

The frown on Mrs. Sommerton's brow cleared away, and she smiled in a manner that was cheering to the heart of her suppliant. He thought it reminded him of the sun breaking through the clouds over the hills beyond the St. Maurice.

"Why, Mr. Mason, how selfishly I've been acting, haven't I? You really must forgive me. It is so funny, too, making you beg for a seat in your own canoe."

"Oh no, it's your canoe - that is, after twelve o'clock to-night. That's when your contract begins."

"The arrangement does not seem to me quite regular; but, then, this is the Canadian woods, and not Boston. But, I want to make my little proviso. I do not wish to be introduced to this man; he must have no excuse for beginning a conversation with me. I don't want to talk to-morrow."

"Heroic resolution," murmured Mason.

"So, I do not wish to see the gentleman until I go into the canoe. You can be conveniently absent. Mrs. Perrault will take me down there; she speaks no English, and it is not likely he can speak French."

"We can arrange that."

"Then it is settled, and all I hope for is a good day to-morrow."

Mrs. Mason sprang up and kissed the fair Bostonian, and Mason felt a sensation of joyous freedom that recalled his youthful days when a half-holiday was announced.

"Oh, it is too good of you," said the elder lady.

"Not a bit of it," whispered Miss Sommerton; "I hate the man before I have seen him."

CHAPTER III.

When John Trenton came in to breakfast, he found his friend Mason waiting for him. That genial gentleman was evidently ill at ease, but he said in an offhand way -

"The ladies have already breakfasted. They are busily engaged in the preparations for the trip, and so you and I can have a snack together, and then we will go and see to the canoe."

After breakfast they went together to the river, and found the canoe and the two half-breeds waiting for them. A couple of rugs were spread on the bottom of the canoe rising over the two slanting boards which served as backs to the lowly seats.

"Now," said Mason with a blush, for he always told a necessary lie with some compunction, "I shall have to go and see to one of my men who was injured in the mill this morning. You had better take your place in the canoe, and wait for your passenger, who, as is usual with ladies, will probably be a little late. I think you should sit in the back seat, as you are the heavier of the two. I presume you remember what I told you about sitting in a canoe? Get in with caution while these two men hold the side of it; sit down carefully, and keep steady, no matter what happens. Perhaps you may as well put your camera here at the back, or in the prow."

"No," said Trenton, "I shall keep it slung over my shoulder. It isn't heavy, and I am always afraid of forgetting it if I leave it anywhere."

Trenton got cautiously into the canoe, while Mason bustled off with a very guilty feeling at his heart. He never thought of blaming Miss Sommerton for the course she had taken, and the dilemma into which she placed him, for he felt that the fault was entirely his own.

John Trenton pulled out his pipe, and, absent-mindedly, stuffed it full of tobacco. Just as he was about to light it, he remembered there was to be a lady in the party, and so with a grimace of disappointment he put the loaded pipe into his pocket again.

It was the most lovely time of the year. The sun was still warm, but the dreaded black fly and other insect pests of the region had disappeared before the sharp frosts that occurred every night. The hilly banks of the St. Maurice were covered with unbroken forest, and "the woods of autumn all around, the vale had put their glory on." Presently Trenton saw Miss Sommerton, accompanied by old Mrs. Perrault, coming over the brow of the hill. He attempted to rise, in order to assist the lady to a seat in the canoe, when the half-breed said in French - :

"Better sit still. It is safer. We will help the lady."

Miss Sommerton was talking rapidly in French - with

Robert Barr

rather overdone eagerness - to Mrs. Perrault. She took no notice of her fellow-voyager as she lightly stepped exactly in the centre of the canoe, and sank down on the rug in front of him, with the ease of one thoroughly accustomed to that somewhat treacherous craft. The two stalwart boatmen - one at the prow, the other at the stern of the canoe - with swift and dexterous strokes, shot it out into the stream. Trenton could not but admire the knowledge of these two men and their dexterous use of it. Here they were on a swiftly flowing river, with a small fall behind them and a tremendous cataract several miles in front, yet these two men, by their knowledge of the currents, managed to work their way up stream with the least possible amount of physical exertion. The St. Maurice at this point is about half a mile wide, with an island here and there, and now and then a touch of rapids. Sometimes the men would dash right across the river to the opposite bank, and there fall in with a miniature Gulf Stream that would carry them onward without exertion. Sometimes they were near the densely wooded shore, sometimes in the center of the river. The half-breed who stood behind Trenton, leant over to him, and whispered -

"You can now smoke if you like, the wind is down stream."

Naturally, Mr. Trenton wished to smoke. The requesting of permission to do so, it struck him, might open the way to conversation. He was not an ardent conversationalist, but it seemed to him rather ridiculous that two persons should thus travel together in a canoe without saying a word to each other.

"I beg your pardon, madam," he began; "but would you

have any objection to my smoking? I am ashamed to confess that I am a slave to the pernicious habit."

There was a moment or two of silence, broken only by the regular dip of the paddle, then Miss Sommerton said, "If you wish to desecrate this lovely spot by smoking, I presume anything I can say will not prevent you."

Trenton was amazed at the rudeness of this reply, and his face flushed with anger. Finally he said, "You must have a very poor opinion of me!"

Miss Sommerton answered tartly, "I have no opinion whatever of you." Then, with womanly inconsistency, she proceeded to deliver her opinion, saying, "A man who would smoke here would smoke in a cathedral."

"I think you are wrong there," said Mr. Trenton, calmly. "I would smoke here, but I would not think of smoking in a cathedral. Neither would I smoke in the humblest log-cabin chapel."

"Sir," said Miss Sommerton, turning partly round, "I came to the St. Maurice for the purpose of viewing its scenery. I hoped to see it alone. I have been disappointed in that, but I must insist on seeing it in silence. I do not wish to carry on a conversation, nor do I wish to enter into a discussion on any subject whatever. I am sorry to have to say this, but it seems to be necessary."

Her remarks so astonished Trenton that he found it impossible to get angrier than he had been when she first spoke. In fact, he found his anger receding rather than augmenting. It was something so entirely new to meet a lady who had such an utter disregard for the rules of politeness that obtain in any civilized society that Mr. Trenton felt he was having a unique and valuable experience.

"Will you pardon me," he said, with apparent submissiveness - "will you pardon me if I disregard your request sufficiently to humbly beg forgiveness for having spoken to you in the first place?"

To this Miss Sommerton made no reply, and the canoe glided along.

After going up the river for a few miles the boatmen came to a difficult part of the voyage. Here the river was divided by an island. The dark waters moved with great swiftness, and with the smoothness of oil, over the concealed rocks, breaking into foam at the foot of the rapids. Now for the first time the Indians had hard work. For quite half an hour they paddled as if in despair, and the canoe moved upward inch by inch. It was not only hard work, but it was work that did not allow of a moment's rest until it was finished, Should the paddles pause but an instant, the canoe would be swept to the bottom of the rapids. When at last the craft floated into the still water above the rapids, the boatmen rested and mopped the perspiration from their brows. Then, without a word, they resumed their steady, easy swing of the paddle. In a short time the canoe drew up at a landing, from which a path ascended the steep hill among the trees. The silence was broken only by the deep, distant, low roar of the Shawenegen Falls. Mr. Trenton sat in his place, while the half-breeds held the canoe steady. Miss Sommerton rose and stepped with firm, self-reliant tread on the landing. Without looking backward she proceeded up the steep hill, and disappeared among the dense foliage. Then Trenton leisurely got out of the canoe.

"You had a hard time of it up that rapid," said the artist in French to the boatmen. "Here is a five-dollar bill to divide when you get down; and, if you bring us safely back, I shall have another ready for you."

The men were profusely grateful, as indeed they had a right to be, for the most they expected was a dollar each as a fee.

"Ah," said the elder, "if we had gentlemen like you to take up every day," and he gave an expressive shrug.

"You shouldn't take such a sordid view of the matter," said the artist. "I should think you would find great pleasure in taking up parties of handsome ladies such as I understand now and then visit the falls."

"Ah," said the boatman, "it is very nice, of course; but, except from Miss Sommerton, we don't get much."

"Really," said the artist; "and who is Miss Sommerton, pray?"

The half-breed nodded up the path.

"Oh, indeed, that is her name. I did not know."

"Yes," said the man, "she is very generous, and she always brings us tobacco in her pocket - good tobacco."

"Tobacco!" cried the artist. "The arrant hypocrite. She gives you tobacco, does she? Did you understand what we were talking about coming up here?"

Robert Barr

The younger half-breed was about to say "Yes," and a gleam of intelligence came into his face; but a frown on the other's brow checked him, and the elder gravely shook his head.

"We do not understand English," he said.

As Trenton walked slowly up the steep hillside, he said to himself, "That young woman does not seem to have the slightest spark of gratitude in her composition. Here I have been good-natured enough, to share my canoe with her, yet she treats me as if I were some low ruffian instead of a gentleman."

As Miss Sommerton was approaching the Shawenegan Falls, she said to herself, "What an insufferable cad that man is? Mr. Mason doubtless told him that he was indebted to me for being allowed to come in the canoe, and yet, although he must see I do not wish to talk with him, he tried to force conversation on me."

Miss Sommerton walked rapidly along the very imperfect woodland path, which was completely shaded by the overhanging trees. After a walk of nearly a mile, the path suddenly ended at the top of a tremendous precipice of granite, and opposite this point the great hillside of tumbling white foam plunged for ever downward. At the foot of the falls the waters flung themselves against the massive granite barrier, and then, turning at a right angle, plunged downward in a series of wild rapids that completely eclipsed in picturesqueness and grandeur and force even the famous rapids at Niagara. Contemplating this incomparable scene, Miss Sommerton forgot all about her objectionable travelling companion. She sat down on a fallen log, placing her sketch-book on her lap, but it lay there idly as, unconscious of the passing time, she gazed dreamily at the great falls and listened to their vibrating deafening roar. Suddenly the consciousness of some one near startled her from her reverie. She sprang to her feet, and had so completely forgotten her companion that she stared at him for a moment in dumb amazement. He stood back some distance from her, and beside him on its slender tripod was placed a natty little camera. Connected with the instantaneous shutter was a long black rubber tube almost as thin as a string. The bulb of this instantaneous attachment Mr. Trenton held in his hand, and the instant Miss Sommerton turned around, the little shutter, as if in defiance of her, gave a snap, and she knew her picture had been taken, and also that she was the principal object in the foreground.

"You have photographed me, sir!" cried the young woman, with her eyes blazing.

"I have photographed the falls, or, at least, I hope I have," replied Trenton.

"But my picture is in the foreground. You must destroy that plate."

"You will excuse me, Miss Sommerton, if I tell you I shall do nothing of the kind. It is very unusual with me to deny the request of a lady, but in this case I must do so. This is the last plate I have, and it may be the one successful picture of the lot. I shall, therefore, not destroy the plate."

"Then, sir, you are not a gentleman!" cried the impetuous young lady, her face aflame with anger.

"I never claimed to be one," answered Trenton, calmly.

"I shall appeal to Mr. Mason; perhaps he has some means of making you understand that you are not allowed to take a lady's photograph without her permission, and in defiance of her wishes."

"Will you allow me to explain why it is unnecessary to destroy the plate? If you understand anything about photography, you must be aware of the fact -"

"I am happy to say I know nothing of photography, and I desire to know nothing of it. I will not hear any explanation from you, sir. You have refused to destroy the plate. That is enough for me. Your conduct to-day has been entirely contemptible. In the first place you have forced yourself, through Mr. Mason, into my company. The canoe was mine for to-day, and you knew it. I granted you permission to come, but I made it a proviso that there should be no conversation. Now, I shall return in the canoe alone, and I shall pay the boatmen to come back for you this evening." With this she swept indignantly past Mr. Trenton, leaving the unfortunate man for the second or third time that day too much dumbfounded to reply. She marched down the path toward the landing. Arriving at the canoe, she told the boatmen they would have to return for Mr. Trenton; that she was going back alone, and she would pay them handsomely for their extra trip. Even the additional pay offered did not seem to quite satisfy the two half-breeds.

"It will be nearly dark before we can get back," grumbled the elder boatman.

"That does not matter," replied Miss Sommerton, shortly.

"But it is dangerous going down the river at night."

"That does not matter," was again the reply.

"But he has nothing -"

"The longer you stand talking here the longer it will be before you get back. If you are afraid for the safety of the gentleman, pray stay here with him and give me the paddle - I will take the boat down alone."

The boatman said nothing more, but shot the canoe out from the landing and proceeded rapidly down the stream.

Miss Sommerton meditated bitterly on the disappointments and annoyances of the day. Once fairly away, conscience began to trouble her, and she remembered that the gentleman so unceremoniously left in the woods without any possibility of getting away was a man whom Mr. Mason, her friend, evidently desired very much to please. Little had been said by the boatmen, merely a brief word of command now and then from the elder who stood in the stern, until they passed down the rapids. Then Miss Sommerton caught a grumbling word in French which made her heart stand still.

"What is that you said?" she cried to the elder boatman.

He did not answer, but solemnly paddled onward.

　　　　　Robert Barr

"Answer me," demanded Miss Sommerton. "What is that you said about the gentleman who went up with us this morning?"

"I said," replied the half-breed, with a grim severity that even the remembrance of gifts of tobacco could not mitigate, "that the canoe belonged to him today."

"How dare you say such a thing! The canoe was mine. Mr. Mason gave it to me. It was mine for to-day."

"I know nothing about that," returned the boatman doggedly; "but I do know that three days ago Mr. Mason came to me with this gentleman's letter in his hand and said, 'Pierre, Mr. Trenton is to have the canoe for Tuesday. See it is in good order, and no one else is to have it for that day.' That is what Mr. Mason said, and when they were down at the canoe this morning, Mr. Mason asked Mr. Trenton if he would let you go up to the falls in his canoe, and he said 'Yes.'"

Miss Sommerton sat there too horrified to speak. A wild resentment against the duplicity of Ed. Mason arose for a moment in her heart, but it speedily sank as she viewed her own conduct in the light of this astounding revelation. She had abused an unknown gentleman like a pickpocket, and had finally gone off with his canoe, leaving him marooned, as it were, to whose courtesy she was indebted for being there at all. Overcome by the thoughts that crowded so quickly upon her, she buried her face in her hands and wept. But this was only for an instant. Raising her head again, with the imperious air characteristic of her, she said to the boatman -

"Turn back at once, please."

"We are almost there now," he answered, amazed at the feminine inconsistency of the command.

"Turn back at once, I say. You are not too tired to paddle up the river again, are you?"

"No, madame," he answered, "but it is so useless; we are almost there. We shall land you, and then the canoe will go up lighter."

"I wish to go with you. Do what I tell you, and I will pay you."

The stolid boatman gave the command; the man at the bow paddled one way, while the man at the stern paddled another, and the canoe swung round upstream again.

CHAPTER IV.

The sun had gone down when Miss Sommerton put her foot once more on the landing.

"We will go and search for him," said the boatman.

"Stay where you are," she commanded, and disappeared swiftly up the path. Expecting to find him still at the falls, she faced the prospect of a good mile of rough walking in the gathering darkness without flinching. But at the brow of the hill, within hearing distance of the landing, she found the man of whom she was in search. In her agony of mind Miss Sommerton had expected to come upon him pacing moodily up and down before the falls, meditating on the ingratitude of womankind. She discovered him in a much less romantic attitude. He was lying at full length below a white birch-tree, with his camera-box under his head for a pillow. It was evident he had seen enough of the Shawenegan Falls for one day, and doubtless, because of the morning's early rising, and the day's long journey, had fallen soundly asleep. His soft felt hat lay on the ground beside him. Miss Sommerton looked at him for a moment, and thought bitterly of Mason's additional perjury in swearing that he was an elderly man. True, his hair was tinged with grey at the temples, but there was nothing elderly about his appearance. Miss Sommerton saw that he was a handsome man, and wondered this had escaped her notice before, forgetting that she had scarcely deigned to look at him. She thought he had spoken to her with inexcusable bluntness at the falls, in refusing to destroy his plate; but she now remembered with compunction that he had made no allusion to his ownership of the boat for that day, while she had boasted that it was hers. She determined to return and send one of the boatmen up to awaken him, but at that moment Trenton suddenly opened his eyes, as a person often does when some one looks at him in his sleep. He sprang quickly to his feet, and put up his hand in bewilderment to remove his hat, but found it wasn't there. Then he laughed uncomfortably, stooping to pick it up again.

"I - I - I wasn't expecting visitors," he stammered -

"Why did you not tell me," she said, "that Mr. Mason had promised you the boat for the day?"

"Good gracious!" cried Trenton, "has Ed. Mason told you that?"

"I have not seen Mr. Mason," she replied; "I found it out by catching an accidental remark made by one of the boat-men. I desire very humbly to apologise to you for my conduct."

"Oh, that doesn't matter at all, I assure you."

"What! My conduct doesn't?"

"No, I didn't mean quite that; but I - Of course, you did treat me rather abruptly; but then, you know, I saw how it was. You looked on me as an interloper, as it were, and I think you were quite justified, you know, in speaking as you did. I am a very poor hand at conversing with ladies, even at my best, and I am not at my best to-day. I had to get up too early, so there is no doubt what I said was said very awkwardly indeed. But it really doesn't matter, you know - that is, it doesn't matter about anything you said."

"I think it matters very much - at least, it matters very much to me. I shall always regret having treated you as I did, and I hope you will forgive me for having done so."

"Oh, that's all right," said Mr. Trenton, swinging his camera over his shoulder. "It is getting dark, Miss Sommerton; I think we should hurry down to the canoe."

As they walked down the hill together, he continued -

"I wish you would let me give you a little lesson in photography, if you don't mind."

"I have very little interest in photography, especially amateur photography," replied Miss Sommerton, with a partial return of her old reserve.

"Oh, I don't wish to make an amateur photographer of you. You sketch very nicely, and -"

"How do you know that?" asked Miss Sommerton, turning quickly towards him: "you have never seen any of my sketches."

"Ah, well," stammered Trenton, "no - that is - you know - are not those water-colours in Mason's house yours?"

"Mr. Mason has some of my sketches. I didn't know you had seen them."

"Well, as I was saying," continued Trenton, "I have no desire to convert you to the beauties of amateur photography. I admit the results in many cases are very bad. I am afraid if you saw the pictures I take myself you would not be much in love with the art. But what I wish to say is in mitigation of my refusal to destroy the plate when you asked me to."

"Oh, I beg you will not mention that, or refer to anything at all I have said to you. I assure you it pains me very much, and you know I have apologised once or twice already."

"Oh, it isn't that. The apology should come from me; but I thought I would like to explain why it is that I did not take your picture, as you thought I did."

"Not take my picture? Why I *saw* you take it. You admitted yourself you took it."

"Well, you see, that is what I want to explain. I took your picture, and then again I didn't take it. This is how it is with amateur photography. Your picture on the plate will be a mere shadow, a dim outline, nothing more. No one can tell who it is. You see, it is utterly impossible to take a dark object and one in pure white at the instantaneous snap. If the picture of the falls is at all correct, as I expect it will be, then your picture will be nothing but a shadow unrecognisable by any one."

"But they do take pictures with the cataract as a

background, do they not? I am sure I have seen photos of groups taken at Niagara Falls; in fact, I have seen groups being posed in public for that purpose, and very silly they looked, I must say. I presume that is one of the things that has prejudiced me so much against the camera."

"Those pictures, Miss Sommerton, are not genuine; they are not at all what they pretend to be. The prints that you have seen are the results of the manipulation of two separate plates, one of the plates containing the group or the person photographed, and the other an instantaneous picture of the falls. If you look closely at one of those pictures you will see a little halo of light or dark around the person photographed. That, to an experienced photographer, shows the double printing. In fact, it is double dealing all round. The deluded victim of the camera imagines that the pictures he gets of the falls, with himself in the foreground, is really a picture of the falls taken at the time he is being photographed. Whereas, in the picture actually taken of him, the falls themselves are hopelessly over-exposed, and do not appear at all on the plate. So with the instantaneous picture I took; there will really be nothing of you on that plate that you would recognise as yourself. That was why I refused to destroy it."

"I am afraid," said Miss Sommerton, sadly, "you are trying to make my punishment harder and harder. I believe in reality you are very cruel. You know how badly I feel about the whole matter, and now even the one little point that apparently gave me any excuse is taken away by your scientific explanation."

"Candidly, Miss Sommerton, I am more of a culprit than you imagine, and I suppose it is the tortures of a guilty conscience that caused me to make this explanation. I shall now confess without reserve. As you sat there with your head in your hand looking at the falls, I deliberately and with malice aforethought took a timed picture, which, if developed, will reveal you exactly as you sat, and which will not show the falls at all."

Miss Sommerton walked in silence beside him, and he could not tell just how angry she might be. Finally he said, "I shall destroy that plate, if you order me to."

Miss Sommerton made no reply, until they were nearly at the canoe. Then she looked up at him with a smile, and said, "I think it a pity to destroy any pictures you have had such trouble to obtain."

"Thank you, Miss Sommerton," said the artist. He helped her into the canoe in the gathering dusk, and then sat down himself. But neither of them saw the look of anxiety on the face of the elder boatman. He knew the River St. Maurice.

CHAPTER V.

From the words the elder boatman rapidly addressed to the younger, it was evident to Mr. Trenton that the half-breed was anxious to pass the rapids before it became very much darker.

The landing is at the edge of comparatively still water. At the bottom of the falls the river turns an acute angle and flows to the west. At the landing it turns with equal abruptness, and flows south.

The short westward section of the river from the falls to the point where they landed is a wild, turbulent rapid, in which no boat can live for a moment. From the Point downwards, although the water is covered with foam, only one dangerous place has to be passed. Toward that spot the stalwart half-breeds bent all their energy in forcing the canoe down with the current. The canoe shot over the darkening rapid with the speed of an arrow. If but one or two persons had been in it, the chances are the passage would have been made in safety. As it was one wrong turn of the paddle by the younger half-breed did the mischief. The bottom barely touched a sharp-pointed hidden rock, and in an instant the canoe was slit open as with a knife.

As he sat there Trenton felt the cold water rise around him with a quickness that prevented his doing anything, even if he had known what to do.

"Sit still!" cried the elder boatman; and then to the younger he shouted sharply, "The shore!"

They were almost under the hanging trees when the four found themselves in the water. Trenton grasped an overhanging branch with one hand, and with the other caught Miss Sommerton by the arm. For a moment it was doubtful whether the branch would hold. The current was very swift, and it threw each of them against the rock bank, and bent the branch down into the water.

"Catch hold of me!" cried Trenton. "Catch hold of my coat; I need both hands."

Miss Sommerton, who had acted with commendable bravery throughout, did as she was directed. Trenton, with his released hand, worked himself slowly up the branch, hand over hand, and finally catching a sapling that grew close to the water's edge, with a firm hold, reached down and helped Miss Sommerton on the bank. Then he slowly drew himself up to a safe position and looked around for any signs of the boatmen. He shouted loudly, but there was no answer.

"Are they drowned, do you think?" asked Miss Sommerton, anxiously.

"No, I don't suppose they are; I don't think you _could_ drown a half-breed. They have done their best to drown us, and as we have escaped I see no reason why they should drown."

"Oh, it's all my fault! all my fault!" wailed Miss Sommerton.

"It is, indeed," answered Trenton, briefly.

She tried to straighten herself up, but, too wet and chilled and limp to be heroic, she sank on a rock and began to cry.

"Please don't do that," said the artist, softly. "Of course I shouldn't have agreed with you. I beg pardon for having done so, but now that we are here, you are not to shirk your share of the duties. I want you to search around and get materials for a fire."

"Search around?" cried Miss Sommerton dolefully.

"Yes, search around. Hunt, as you Americans say. You have got us into this scrape, so I don't propose you shall sit calmly by and not take any of the consequences."

"Do you mean to insult me, Mr. Trenton, now that I am helpless?"

"If it is an insult to ask you to get up and gather some wood and bring it here, then I do mean to insult you most emphatically. I shall gather some, too, for we shall need a quantity of it."

Miss Sommerton rose indignantly, and was on the point of threatening to leave the place, when a moment's reflection showed her that she didn't know where to go, and remembering she was not as brave in the darkness and in the woods as in Boston, she meekly set about the search for dry twigs and sticks.

Flinging down the bundle near the heap Trenton had already collected, the young woman burst into a laugh.

"Do you see anything particularly funny in the situation?" asked Trenton, with chattering teeth. "I confess I do not."

"The funniness of the situation is that we should gather wood, when, if there is a match in your pocket, it must be so wet as to be useless."

"Oh, not at all. You must remember I come from a very damp climate, and we take care of our matches there. I have been in the water before now on a tramp, and my matches are in a silver case warranted to keep out the wet." As he said this Trenton struck a light, and applied it to the small twigs and dry autumn leaves. The flames flashed up through the larger sticks, and in a very few moments a cheering fire was blazing, over which Trenton threw armful after armful of the wood he had collected.

"Now," said the artist, "if you will take off what outer wraps you have on, we can spread them here, and dry them. Then if you sit, first facing the fire and next with your back to it, and maintain a sort of rotatory motion, it will not be long before you are reasonably dry and warm."

Miss Sommerton laughed, but there was not much merriment in her laughter.

"Was there ever anything so supremely ridiculous?" she said. "A gentleman from England gathering sticks, and a lady from Boston gyrating before the fire. I am glad you are not a newspaper man, for you might be tempted to write about the situation for some sensational paper."

"How do you know I am not a journalist?"

"Well, I hope you are not. I thought you were a photographer."

"Oh, not a professional photographer, you know."

"I am sorry; I prefer the professional to the amateur."

"I like to hear you say that."

"Why? It is not very complimentary, I am sure."

"The very reason I like to hear you say it. If you were complimentary I would be afraid you were going to take a chill and be ill after this disaster; but now that you are yourself again, I have no such fear."

"Myself again!" blazed the young woman. "What do you know about me? How do you know whether I am myself or somebody else? I am sure our acquaintance has been very short."

"Counted by time, yes. But an incident like this, in the wilderness, does more to form a friendship, or the reverse, than years of ordinary acquaintance in Boston or London. You ask how I know that you are yourself. Shall I tell you?"

"If you please."

"Well, I imagine you are a young lady who has been spoilt. I think probably you are rich, and have had a good deal of your own way in this world. In fact, I take it for granted that you have never met any one who frankly told you your faults. Even if such good fortune had been yours, I doubt if you would have profited by it. A snub would have been the reward of the courageous person who told Miss Sommerton her failings."

"I presume you have courage enough to tell me my faults without the fear of a snub before your eyes."

"I have the courage, yes. You see I have already, received the snub three or four times, and it has lost its terrors for me."

"In that case, will you be kind enough to tell me what you consider my faults?"

"If you wish me to."

"I do wish it."

"Well, then, one of them is inordinate pride."

"Do you think pride a fault?"

"It is not usually reckoned one of the virtues."

"In this country, Mr. Trenton, we consider that every person should have a certain amount of pride,"

"A certain amount may be all right. It depends entirely on how much the certain amount is."

"Well, now for fault No. 2."

"Fault No. 2 is a disregard on your part for the feelings of others. This arises, I imagine, partly from fault No. 1. You are in the habit of classing the great mass of the public very much beneath you in intellect and other qualities, and you forget that persons whom you may perhaps dislike, have feelings which you have no right to ignore."

"I presume you refer to this morning," said Miss Sommerton, seriously. "I apologised for that two or three times, I think. I have always understood that a gentleman regards an apology from another gentleman as blotting out the original offence. Why should he not regard it in the same light when it comes from a woman?"

"Oh, now you are making a personal matter of it. I am talking in an entirely impersonal sense. I am merely giving you, with brutal rudeness, opinions formed on a very short acquaintance. Remember, I have done so at your own request."

"I am very much obliged to you, I am sure. I think you are more than half right. I hope the list is not much longer."

"No, the list ends there. I suppose you imagine that I am one of the rudest men you ever met?"

"No, we generally expect rudeness from Englishmen."

"Oh, do you really? Then I am only keeping up the reputation my country-men have already acquired in America. Have you had the pleasure of meeting a rude Englishman before?"

"No, I can't say that I have. Most Englishmen I have met have been what we call very gentlemanly indeed. But the rudest letter I ever received was from an Englishman; not only rude, but ungrateful, for I had bought at a very high price one of his landscapes. He was John Trenton, the artist, of London. Do you know him?"

"Yes," hesitated Trenton, "I know him. I may say I know him very well. In fact, he is a namesake of mine."

"Why, how curious it is I had never thought of that. Is your first name J -, the same as his?"

"Yes."

"Not a relative, is he?"

"Well, no. I don't think I can call him a relative. I don't know that I can even go so far as to call him my friend, but he is an acquaintance."

"Oh, tell me about him," cried Miss Sommerton, enthusiastically. "Heis one of the Englishmen I have longed very much to meet."

"Then you forgave him his rude letter?"

"Oh, I forgave that long ago. I don't know that it was rude, after all. It was truthful. I presume the truth offended me."

"Well," said Trenton, "truth has to be handled very delicately, or it is apt to give offence. You bought a landscape of his, did you? Which one, do you remember?"

"It was a picture of the Thames valley."

"Ah, I don't recall it at the moment. A rather hackneyed subject, too. Probably he sent it to America because he couldn't sell it in England."

"Oh, I suppose you think we buy anything here that the English refuse, I beg to inform you this picture had a place in the Royal Academy, and was very highly spoken of by the critics. I bought it in England."

"Oh yes, I remember it now, 'The Thames at Sonning.' Still, it was ahackneyed subject, although reasonably well treated."

"Reasonably well! I think it one of the finest landscape pictures of the century."

"Well, in that at least Trenton would agree with you."

"He is very conceited, you mean?"

"Even his enemies admit that."

"I don't believe it. I don't believe a man of such talent could be so conceited."

"Then, Miss Sommerton, allow me to say you have very little knowledge of human nature. It is only reasonable that a great man should know he is a great man. Most of our great men are conceited. I would like to see Trenton's letter to you. I could then have a good deal of amusement at his expense when I get back."

"Well, in that case I can assure you that you will never see the letter."

"Ah, you destroyed it, did you?"

"Not for that reason."

"Then you *did* destroy it?"

"I tore it up, but on second thoughts I pasted it together again, and have it still."

"In that case, why should you object to showing me the letter?"

"Well, because I think it rather unusual for a lady to be asked by a gentleman show him a letter that has been written to her by another gentleman."

"In matters of the heart that is true; but in matters of art it is not."

"Is that intended for a pun?"

"It is as near to one as I ever allow myself to come, I should like very much to see Mr. Trenton's letter. It was probably brutally rude. I know the man, you see."

"It was nothing of the sort," replied Miss Sommerton, hotly. "It was a truthful, well-meant letter."

"And yet you tore it up?"

"But that was the first impulse. The pasting it together was the apology."

Robert Barr

"And you will not show it to me?"

"No, I will not."

"Did you answer it?"

"I will tell you nothing more about it. I am sorry I spoke of the letter at all. You don't appreciate Mr. Trenton's work."

"Oh, I beg your pardon, I do. He has no greater admirer in England than I am - except himself, of course."

"I suppose it makes no difference to you to know that I don't like a remark like that."

"Oh, I thought it would please you. You see, with the exception of myself, Mr. Trenton is about the rudest man in England. In fact, I begin to suspect it was Mr. Trenton's letter that led you to a wholesale condemning of the English race, for you admit the Englishmen you have met were not rude."

"You forget I have met you since then."

"Well bowled, as we say in cricket."

"Has Mr. Trenton many friends in London?"

"Not a great number. He is a man who sticks rather closely to his work, and, as I said before, he prides himself on telling the truth. That doesn't do in London any more than it does in Boston."

"Well, I honour him for it."

"Oh, certainly; everybody does in the abstract. But it is not a quality that tends to the making or the keeping of friends, you know."

"If you see Mr. Trenton when you return, I wish you would tell him there is a lady in America who is a friend of his; and if he has any pictures the people over there do not appreciate, ask him to send them to Boston, and his friend will buy them."

"Then you must be rich, for his pictures bring very good prices, even in England."

"Yes," said Miss Sommerton, "I am rich."

"Well, I suppose it's very jolly to be rich," replied the artist, with a sigh.

"You are not rich, then, I imagine?"

"No, I am not. That is, not compared with your American fortunes. I have enough of money to let me roam around the world if I wish to, and get half drowned in the St. Maurice River."

"Oh, is it not strange that we have heard nothing from those boatmen? You surely don't imagine they could have been drowned?"

"I hardly think so. Still, it is quite possible."

"Oh, don't say that; it makes me feel like a murderer."

"Well, I think it was a good deal your fault, don't you know." Miss Sommerton looked at him.

"Have I not been punished enough already?" she said.

"For the death of two men - if they are dead? Bless me! no. Do you imagine for a moment there is any relation between the punishment and the fault?"

Miss Sommertan buried her face in her hands.

"Oh, I take that back," said Trenton. "I didn't mean to say such a thing."

"It is the truth - it is the truth!" wailed the young woman. "Do you honestly think they did not reach the shore?"

"Of course they did. If you want to know what has happened, I'll tell you exactly, and back my opinion by a bet if you like. An Englishman is always ready to back his opinion, you know. Those two men swam with the current until they came to some landing-place. They evidently think we are drowned. Nevertheless, they are now making their way through the woods to the settlement. Then comes the hubbub. Mason will stir up the neighbourhood, and the men who are back from the woods with the other canoes will be roused and pressed into service, and some time to-night we will be rescued."

"Oh, I hope that is the case," cried Miss Sommerton, looking brightly at him.

"It is the case. Will you bet about it?"

"I never bet," said Miss Sommerton.

"Ah, well, you miss a good deal of fun then. You see I

am a bit of a mind reader. I can tell just about where the men are now."

"I don't believe much in mind reading."

"Don't you? Shall I give you a specimen of it? Take that letter we have spoken so much about. If you think it over in your mind I will read you the letter - not word for word, perhaps, but I shall give you gist of it, at least."

"Oh, impossible!"

"Do you remember it?"

"I have it with me."

"Oh, have you? Then, if you wish to preserve it, you should spread it out upon the ground to dry before the fire."

"There is no need of my producing the letter," replied Miss Sommerton; "I remember every word it."

"Very well, just think it over in your mind, and see if I cannot repeat it. Are you thinking about it?"

"Yes, I am thinking about it."

"Here goes, then. 'Miss Edith Sommerton -'"

"Wrong," said that young lady.

"The Sommerton is right, is it not?"

"Yes, but the first name is not."

"What is it, then?"

"I shall not tell you."

"Oh, very well. Miss Sommerton, - 'I have some hesitation in answering your letter.' Oh, by the way, I forgot the address. That is the first sentence of the letter, but the address is some number which I cannot quite see, 'Beacon Street, Boston.' Is there any such street in that city?"

"There is," said Miss Sommerton. "What a question to ask."

"Ah, then Beacon Street is one of the principal streets, is it?"

"One of them? It is *the* street. It is Boston."

"Very good. I will now proceed with the letter. 'I have some hesitation in answering your letter, because the sketches you send are so bad, that it seems to me no one could seriously forward them to an artist for criticism. However, if you really desire criticism, and if the pictures are sent in good faith, I may say I see in them no merit whatever, not even good drawing; while the colours are put on in a way that would seem to indicate you have not yet learned the fundamental principle of mixing the paints. If you are thinking of earning a livelihood with your pencil, I strongly advise you to abandon the idea. But if you are a lady of leisure and wealth, I suppose there is no harm in your continuing as long as you see fit. - Yours truly, JOHN TRENTON.'"

Miss Sommerton, whose eyes had opened wider and

wider as this reading went on, said sharply -

"He has shown you the letter. You have seen it before it was sent."

"I admit that," said the artist.

"Well - I will believe all you like to say about Mr. John Trenton."

"Now, stop a moment; do not be too sweeping in your denunciation of him. I know that Mr. Trenton showed the letter to no one."

"Why, I thought you said a moment ago that he showed it to you."

"He did. Yet no one but himself saw the letter."

The young lady sprang to her feet.

"Are you, then, John Trenton, the artist?"

"Miss Sommerton, I have to plead guilty."

CHAPTER VI.

Miss Eva Sommerton and Mr. John Trenton stood on opposite sides of the blazing fire and looked at each other. A faint smile hovered around the lips of the artist, but Miss Sommerton's face was very serious. She was the first to speak.

"It seems to me," she said, "that there is something about all this that smacks of false pretences."

"On my part, Miss Sommerton?"

"Certainly on your part. You must have known all along that I was the person who had written the letter to you. I think, when you found that out, you should have spoken of it."

"Then you do not give me credit for the honesty of speaking now. You ought to know that I need not have spoken at all, unless I wished to be very honest about the matter."

"Yes, there is that to be said in your favour, of course."

"Well, Miss Sommerton, I hope you will consider anything that happens to be in my favour. You see, we are really old friends, after all."

"Old enemies, you mean."

"Oh, I don't know about that. I would rather look on myself as your friend than your enemy."

"The letter you wrote me was not a very friendly one."

"I am not so sure. We differ on that point, you know."

"I am afraid we differ on almost every point."

"No, I differ with you there again. Still, I must admit I would prefer being your enemy -"

"To being my friend?" said Miss Sommerton, quickly.

"No, to being entirely indifferent to you."

"Really, Mr. Trenton, we are getting along very rapidly, are we not?" said the young lady, without looking up at him.

"Now, I am pleased to be able to agree with you there, Miss Sommerton. As I said before, an incident like this does more to ripen acquaintance or friendship, or -" The young man hesitated, and did not complete his sentence.

"Well," said the artist, after a pause, "which is it to be, friends or enemies?"

"It shall be exactly as you say," she replied.

"If you leave the choice to me, I shall say friends. Let us shake hands on that."

She held out her hand frankly to him as he crossed over to her side, and as he took it in his own, a strange thrill passed through him, and acting on the impulse of the moment, he drew her toward him and kissed her.

"How dare you!" she cried, drawing herself indignantly from him. "Do you think I am some backwoods girl who is flattered by your preference after a day's acquaintance?"

"Not a day's acquaintance, Miss Sommerton - a year, two years, ten years. In fact, I feel as though I had known you all my life."

"You certainly act as if you had. I did think for some time past that you were a gentleman. But you take advantage now of my unprotected position."

"Miss Sommerton, let me humbly apologise!"

"I shall not accept your apology. It cannot be apologised for. I must ask you not to speak to me again until Mr. Mason comes. You may consider yourself very fortunate when I tell you I shall say nothing of what has passed to Mr. Mason when he arrives."

John Trenton made no reply, but gathered another armful of wood and flung it on the fire.

Miss Sommerton sat very dejectedly looking at the embers.

For half an hour neither of them said anything.

Suddenly Trenton jumped up and listened intently.

"What is it?" cried Miss Sommerton, startled by his action.

"Now," said Trenton, "that is unfair. If I am not to be allowed to speak to you, you must not ask me any questions."

"I beg your pardon," said Miss Sommerton, curtly.

"But really I wanted to say something, and I wanted you to be the first to break the contract imposed. May I say what I wish to? I have just thought about something."

"If you have thought of anything that will help us out of our difficulty, I shall be very glad to hear it indeed."

"I don't know that it will help us *out* of our difficulties, but I think it will help us now that we're *in* them. You know, I presume, that my camera, like John Brown's knapsack, was strapped on my back, and that it is one of the few things rescued from the late disaster?"

He paused for a reply, but she said nothing. She evidently was not interested in his camera.

"Now, that camera-box is water-tight. It is really a very natty arrangement, although you regard it so scornfully."

He paused a second time, but there was no reply.

"Very well; packed in that box is, first the camera, then the dry plates, but most important of all, there are at least two or three very nice Three Rivers sandwiches. What do you say to our having supper?"

Miss Sommerton smiled in spite of herself, and Trenton busily unstrapped the camera-box, pulled out the little instrument, and fished up from the bottom a neatly-folded white table-napkin, in which were wrapped several sandwiches.

"Now," he continued, "I have a folding drinking-cup and a flask of sherry. It shows how absent-minded I am, for I ought to have thought of the wine long ago. You should have had a glass of sherry the moment we landed here. By the way, I wanted to say, and I say it now in case I shall forget it, that when I ordered you so unceremoniously to go around picking up sticks for the fire, it was not because I needed assistance, but to keep you, if possible, from getting a chill."

"Very kind of you," remarked Miss Sommerton.

But the Englishman could not tell whether she meant just what she said or not.

"I wish you would admit that you are hungry. Have you had anything to eat to-day?"

"I had, I am ashamed to confess," she answered. "I took lunch with me and I ate it coming down in the canoe. That was what troubled me about you. I was afraid you had eaten nothing all day, and I wished to offer you some lunch when we were in the canoe, but scarcely liked to. I thought we would soon reach the settlement. I am very glad you have sandwiches with you."

"How little you Americans really know of the great British nation, after all. Now, if there is one thing more than another that an Englishman looks after, it is the commissariat."

After a moment's silence he said -

"Don't you think, Miss Sommerton, that notwith-
standing any accident or disaster, or misadventure that
may have happened, we might get back at least on the
old enemy footing again? I would like to apologise" -
he paused for a moment, and added, "for the letter I
wrote you ever so many years ago."

"There seem to be too many apologies between us,"
she replied. "I shall neither give nor take any more."

"Well," he answered, "I think after all that is the best
way. You ought, to treat me rather kindly though,
because you are the cause of my being here."

"That is one of the many things I have apologised for.
You surely do not wish to taunt me with it again?"

"Oh, I don't mean the recent accident. I mean being
here in America. Your sketches of the Shawenegan
Falls, and your description of the Quebec district,
brought me out to America; and, added to that - I
expected to meet you."

"To meet me?"

"Certainly. Perhaps you don't know that I called at
Beacon Street, and found you were from home - with
friends in Canada, they said - and I want to say, in self-
defence, that I came very well introduced. I brought
letters to people in Boston of the most undoubted
respectability, and to people in New York, who are as
near the social equals of the Boston people as it is

possible for mere New York persons to be. Among other letters of introduction I had two to you. I saw the house in Beacon Street. So, you see, I have no delusions about your being a backwoods girl, as you charged me with having a short time since."

"I would rather not refer to that again, if you please."

"Very well. Now, I have one question to ask you - one request to make. Have I your permission to make it?"

"It depends entirely on what your request is."

"Of course, in that case you cannot tell until I make it. So I shall now make my request, and I want you to remember, before you refuse it, that you are indebted to me for supper. Miss Sommerton, give me a plug of tobacco."

Miss Sommerton stood up in dumb amazement.

"You see," continued the artist, paying no heed to her evident resentment, "I have lost my tobacco in the marine disaster, but luckily I have my pipe. I admit the scenery is beautiful here, if we could only see it; but darkness is all around, although the moon is rising. It can therefore be no desecration for me to smoke a pipeful of tobacco, and I am sure the tobacco you keep will be the very best that can be bought. Won't you grant my request, Miss Sommerton?"

At first Miss Sommerton seemed to resent the audacity of this request. Then a conscious light came into her face, and instinctively her hand pressed the side of her dress where her pocket was supposed to be.

"Now," said the artist, "don't deny that you have the tobacco. I told you I was a bit of a mind reader, and besides, I have been informed that young ladies in America are rarely without the weed, and that they only keep the best."

The situation was too ridiculous for Miss Sommerton to remain very long indignant about it. So she put her hand in her pocket and drew out a plug of tobacco, and with a bow handed it to the artist.

"Thanks," he replied; "I shall borrow a pipeful and give you back the remainder. Have you ever tried the English birdseye? I assure you it is a very nice smoking tobacco."

"I presume," said Miss Sommerton, "the boatmen told you I always gave them some tobacco when I came up to see the falls?"

"Ah, you will doubt my mind-reading gift. Well, honestly, they did tell me, and I thought perhaps you might by good luck have it with you now. Besides, you know, wasn't there the least bit of humbug about your objection to smoking as we came up the river? If you really object to smoking, of course I shall not smoke now."

"Oh, I haven't the least objection to it. I am sorry I have not a good cigar to offer you."

"Thank you. But this is quite as acceptable. We rarely use plug tobacco in England, but I find some of it in this country is very good indeed."

"I must confess," said Miss Sommerton, "that I have

very little interest in the subject of tobacco. But I cannot see why we should not have good tobacco in this country. We grow it here."

"That's so, when you come to think of it," answered the artist.

Trenton sat with his back against the tree, smoking in a meditative manner, and watching the flicker of the firelight on the face of his companion, whose thoughts seemed to be concentrated on the embers.

"Miss Sommerton," he said at last, "I would like permission to ask you a second question.

"You have it," replied that lady, without looking up.

"But to prevent disappointment, I may say this is all the tobacco I have. The rest I left in the canoe when I went up to the falls."

"I shall try to bear the disappointment as well as I may. But in this case the question is of a very different nature. I don't know just exactly how to put it. You may have noticed that I am rather awkward when it comes to saying the right thing at the right time. I have not been much accustomed to society, and I am rather a blunt man."

"Many persons," said Miss Sommerton with some severity, "pride themselves on their bluntness. They seem to think it an excuse for saying rude things. There is a sort of superstition that bluntness and honesty go together."

"Well, that is not very encouraging, However, I do not

pride myself on my bluntness, but rather regret it. I was merely stating a condition of things, not making a boast. In this instance I imagine. I can show that honesty is the accompaniment. The question I wished to ask was something like this: Suppose I had had the chance to present to you my letters of introduction, and suppose that we had known each other for some time, and suppose that everything had been very conventional, instead of somewhat unconventional; supposing all this, would you have deemed a recent action of mine so unpardonable as you did a while ago?"

"You said you were not referring to smoking,"

"Neither am I. I am referring to my having kissed you. There's bluntness for you."

"My dear sir," replied Miss Sommerton, shading her face with her hand, "you know nothing whatever of me."

"That is rather evading the question."

"Well, then, I know nothing whatever of you."

"That is the second evasion. I am taking it for granted that we each know something of the other."

"I should think it would depend entirely on how the knowledge influenced each party in the case. It is such, a purely supposititious state of things that I cannot see how I can answer your question. I suppose you have heard the adage about not crossing a bridge until you come to it."

"I thought it was a stream."

"Well, a stream then. The principle is the same.'"

"I was afraid I would not be able to put the question in a way to make you understand it. I shall now fall back on my bluntness again, and with this question, are you betrothed?"

"We generally call it engaged in this country."

"Then I shall translate my question into the language of the country, and ask if -"

"Oh, don't ask it, please. I shall answer before you do ask it by saying, No. I do not know why I should countenance your bluntness, as you call it, by giving you an answer to such a question; but I do so on condition that the question is the last."

"But the second question cannot be the last. There is always the third reading of a bill. The auctioneer usually cries, 'Third and last time,' not 'Second and last time,' and the banns of approaching marriage are called out three times. So, you see, I have the right to ask you one more question."

"Very well. A person may sometimes have the right to do a thing, and yet be very foolish in exercising that right."

"I accept your warning," said the artist, "and reserve my right."

"What time is it, do you think?" she asked him.

"I haven't the least idea," he replied; "my watch has stopped. That case was warranted to resist water, but I doubt if it has done so."

"Don't you think that if the men managed to save themselves they would have been here by this time?"

"I am sure I don't know. I have no idea of the distance. Perhaps they may have taken it for granted we are drowned, and so there is one chance in a thousand that they may not come back at all."

"Oh, I do not think such a thing is possible. The moment Mr. Mason heard of the disaster he would come without delay, no matter what he might believe the result of the accident to be."

"Yes, I think you are right. I shall try to get out on this point and see if I can discover anything of them. The moon now lights up the river, and if they are within a reasonable distance I think I can see them from this point of rock."

The artist climbed up on the point, which projected over the river. The footing was not of the safest, and Miss Sommerton watched him with some anxiety as he slipped and stumbled and kept his place by holding on to the branches of the overhanging trees.

"Pray be careful, Mr. Trenton," she said; "remember you are over the water there, and it is very swift."

"The rocks seem rather slippery with the dew," answered the artist; "but I am reasonably surefooted."

"Well, please don't take any chances; for, disagreeable as you are, I don't wish to be left here alone."

"Thank you, Miss Sommerton."

The artist stood on the point of rock, and, holding by a branch of a tree, peered out over the river.

"Oh, Mr. Trenton, don't do that!" cried the young lady, with alarm. "Please come back."

"Say 'John,' then," replied the gentleman.

"Oh, Mr. Trenton, don't!" she cried as he leaned still further over the water, straining the branch to its utmost.

"Say 'John.'"

"Mr. Trenton."

"'John.'"

The branch cracked ominously as Trenton leaned yet a little further.

"John!" cried the young lady, sharply, "cease your fooling and come down from that rock."

The artist instantly recovered his position, and, coming back, sprang down to the ground again.

Miss Sommerton drew back in alarm; but Trenton merely put his hands in his pockets, and said -

"Well, Eva, I came back because you called me."

"It was a case of coercion," she said. "You English are too fond of coercion. We Americans are against it."

"Oh, I am a Home Ruler, if you are," replied the artist. "Miss Eva, I am going to risk my third and last question, and I shall await the answer with more anxiety than I ever felt before in my life. The question is this: Will -"

"Hello! there you are. Thank Heaven! I was never so glad to see anybody in my life," cried the cheery voice of Ed. Mason, as he broke through the bushes towards them.

Trenton looked around with anything but a welcome on his brow. If Mason had never been so glad in his life to see anybody, it was quite evident his feeling was not entirely reciprocated by the artist.

"How the deuce did you get here?" asked Trenton. "I was just looking for you down the river."

"Well, you see, we kept pretty close to the shore. I doubt if you could have seen us. Didn't you hear us shout?"

"No, we didn't hear anything. We didn't hear them shout, did we, Miss Sommerton?"

"No," replied that young woman, looking at the dying fire, whose glowing embers seemed to redden her face.

"Why, do you know," said Mason, "it looks as if you had been quarrelling. I guess I came just in the nick of time."

"You are always just in time, Mr. Mason," said Miss Sommerton. "For we were quarrelling, as you say. The subject of the quarrel is which of us was rightful owner of that canoe."

Mason laughed heartily, while Miss Sommerton frowned at him with marked disapprobation.

"Then you found me out, did you? Well, I expected you would before the day was over. You see, it isn't often that I have to deal with two such particular people in the same day. Still, I guess the ownership of the
canoe doesn't amount to much now. I'll give it to the one who finds it."

"Oh, Mr. Mason," cried Miss Sommerton, "did the two men escape all right?"

"Why, certainly, I have just been giving them 'Hail Columbia,' because they didn't come back to you; but you see, a little distance down, the bank gets very steep - so much so that it is impossible to climb it, and then the woods here are thick and hard to work a person's way through. So they thought it best to come down and tell me, and we have brought two canoes up with us."

"Does Mrs. Mason know of the accident?"

"No, she doesn't; but she is just as anxious as if she did. She can't think what in the world keeps you."

"She doesn't realise," said the artist, "what strong attractions the Shawenegan Falls have for people alive to the beauties of nature."

"Well," said Mason, "we mustn't stand here talking. You must be about frozen to death." Here he shouted to one of the men to come up and put out the fire.

"Oh, don't bother," said the artist; "it will soon burn out."

"Oh yes," put in Ed. Mason; "and if a wind should happen to rise in the night, where would my pine forest be? I don't propose to have a whole section of the country burnt up to commemorate the quarrel between you two."

The half-breed flung the biggest brand into the river, and speedily trampled out the rest, carrying up some water in his hat to pour on the centre of the fire. This done, they stepped into the canoe and were soon on their way down the river. Reaching the landing, the artist gave his hand to Miss Sommerton and aided her out on the bank.

"Miss Sommerton," he whispered to her, "I intended to sail to-morrow. I shall leave it for you to say whether I shall go or not."

"You will not sail," said Miss Sommerton promptly.

"Oh, thank you," cried the artist; "you do not know how happy that makes me."

"Why should it?"

"Well, you know what I infer from your answer."

"My dear sir, I said that you would not sail, and you will not, for this reason: To sail you require to catch to-night's train for Montreal, and take the train from there to New York to get your boat. You cannot catch to-night's train, and, therefore, cannot get to your steamer. I never before saw a man so glad to miss his train or his boat. Good-night, Mr. Trenton. Good-night, Mr. Mason," she cried aloud to that gentleman, as she disappeared toward the house.

"You two appear to be quite friendly," said Mr. Mason to the artist. "Do we? Appearances are deceitful. I really cannot tell at this moment whether we are friends or enemies."

"Well, not enemies, I am sure. Miss Eva is a very nice girl when you understand her."

"Do *you* understand her?" asked the artist.

"I can't say that I do. Come to think of it, I don't think anybody does."

"In that case, then, for all practical purposes, she might just as well not be a nice girl."

"Ah, well, you may change your opinion some day - when you get better acquainted with her," said Mason, shaking hands with his friend. "And now that you have missed your train, anyhow, I don't suppose you care for a very early start to-morrow. Good-night."

CHAPTER VII.

After Trenton awoke next morning he thought the situation over very calmly, and resolved to have question number three answered that day if possible.

When called to breakfast he found Ed Mason at the head of the table.

"Shan't we wait for the ladies?" asked the artist.

"I don't think we'd better. You see we might have to wait quite a long time. I don't know when Miss Sommerton will be here again, and it will be a week at least before Mrs. Mason comes back. They are more than half-way to Three Rivers by this time."

"Good gracious!" cried Trenton, abashed; "why didn't you call me? I should have liked very much to have accompanied them."

"Oh, they wouldn't hear of your being disturbed; and besides, Mr. Trenton, our American ladies are quite in the habit of looking after themselves. I found that out long ago."

"I suppose there is nothing for it but get out my backboard and get back to Three Rivers."

Robert Barr

"Oh, I dismissed your driver long ago," said the lumberman. "I'll take you there in my buggy. I am going out to Three Rivers to-day anyhow."

"No chance of overtaking the ladies?" asked Trenton.

"I don't think so. We may overtake Mrs. Mason but I imagine Miss Sommerton will be either at Quebec or Montreal before we reach Three Rivers. I don't know in which direction she is going. You seem to be somewhat interested in that young lady. Purely artistic admiration, I presume. She is rather a striking girl. Well, you certainly have made the most of your opportunities. Let's see, you have known her now for quite a long while. Must be nearly twenty-four hours."

"Oh, don't underestimate it, Mason; quite thirty-six hours at least."

"So long as that? Ah, well, I don't wish to discourage you; but I wouldn't be too sure of her if I were you."

"Sure of her! Why, I am not sure of anything."

"Well, that is the proper spirit. You Englishmen are rather apt to take things for granted. I think you would make a mistake in this case if you were too sure. You are not the only man who has tried to awaken the interest of Miss Sommerton of Boston."

"I didn't suppose that I was. Nevertheless, I am going to Boston."

"Well, it's a nice town," said Mason, with a noncommittal air. "It hasn't the advantages of Three Rivers, of course; but still it is a very attractive place in some respects."

"In some respects, yes," said the artist.

*   *   *   *   *

Two days later Mr. John Trenton called at the house on Beacon Street.

"Miss Sommerton is not at home," said the servant. "She is in Canada somewhere."

And so Mr. Trenton went back to his hotel.

The artist resolved to live quietly in Boston until Miss Sommerton returned. Then the fateful number three could be answered. He determined not to present any of his letters of introduction. When he came to Boston first, he thought he would like to see something of society, of the art world in that city, if there was an art world, and of the people; but he had come and gone without being invited anywhere, and now he anticipated no trouble in living a quiet life, and thinking occasionally over the situation. But during his absence it appeared Boston had awakened to the fact that in its midst had resided a real live artist of prominence from the other side, and nothing had been done to overcome his prejudices, and show him that, after all, the real intellectual centre of the world was not London, but the capital of Massachusetts.

The first day he spent in his hotel he was called upon by a young gentleman whose card proclaimed him a reporter on one of the large daily papers.

"You are Mr. Trenton, the celebrated English artist, are

you not?"

"My name is Trenton, and by profession I am an artist. But I do not claim the adjective, 'celebrated.'"

"All right. You are the man I am after. Now, I should like to know what you think of the art movement in America?"

"Well, really, I have been in America but a very short time, and during that time I have had no opportunity of seeing the work of your artists or of visiting any collections, so you see I cannot give an opinion."

"Met any of our American artists?"

"I have in Europe, yes. Quite a number of them, and very talented gentlemen some of them are, too."

"I suppose Europe lays over this country in the matter of art, don't it?"

"I beg your pardon."

"Knocks the spots out of us in pictures?"

"I don't know that I quite follow you. Do you mean that we produce pictures more rapidly than you do here?"

"No, I just mean the whole *tout ensemble* of the thing. They are 'way ahead of us, are they not, in art?"

"Well, you see, as I said before - really, I am not in a position to make any comparison, because I am entirely ignorant of American painting. It seems to me that certain branches of art ought to flourish here. There is no country in the world with grander scenery than America."

"Been out to the Rockies?"

"Where is that?"

"To the Rocky Mountains?"

"Oh no, no. You see I have been only a few weeks in this country. I have confined my attention to Canada mainly, the Quebec region and around there, although I have been among the White Mountains, and the Catskills, and the Adirondacks."

"What school of art do you belong to?"

"School? Well, I don't know that I belong to any. May I ask if you are a connoisseur in art matters. Are you the art critic of your journal?"

"Me? No - oh no. I don't know the first darn thing about it. That's why they sent me."

"Well, I should have thought, if he wished to get anything worth publishing, your editor would have sent somebody who was at least familiar with the subject he has to write about."

"I dare say; but, that ain't the way to get snappy articles written. You take an art man, now, for instance; he's prejudiced. He thinks one school is all right, and another school isn't; and he is apt to work in his own fads. Now, if our man liked the French school, and despised the English school, or the German school, if there is one, or the Italian school, whatever it happened to be, and you went against that; why, don't you see, he would think you didn't know anything, and write you up that way. Now, I am perfectly unprejudiced. I want to write a good readable article, and I don't care a hang which school is the best or the worst, or anything else about it."

"Ah! I see. Well, in that case, you certainly approach your work without bias."

"You bet I do. Now, who do you think is the best painter in England?"

"In what line?"

"Well, in any line. Who stands ahead? Who's the leader? Who tops them all? Who's the Raphael?"

"I don't know that we have any Raphael? We have good painters each in his own branch."

"Isn't there one, in your opinion, that is 'way ahead of all the rest?"

"Well, you see, to make an intelligent comparison, you have to take into consideration the specialty of the painter. You could hardly compare Alma Tadema, for instance, with Sir John Millais, or Sir Frederic Leighton with Hubert Herkomer, or any of them with some of your own painters. Each has his specialty, and each stands at the head of it."

"Then there is no one man in England like Old Man Rubens, or Van Dyke, or those other fellows, I forget their names, who are head and shoulders above everybody else? Sort of Jay Gould in art, you know."

"No, I wouldn't like to say there is. In fact, all of your questions require some consideration. Now, if you will write them down for me, and give me time to think them over, I will write out such answers as occur to me. It would be impossible for me to do justice to myself, or to art, or to your paper, by attempting to answer questions off-hand in this way."

"Oh, that's too slow for our time here. You know this thing comes out to-morrow morning, and I have got to do a column and a half of it. Sometimes, you know, it is very difficult; but you are different from most Englishmen I have talked with. You speak right out, and you talk to a fellow. I can make a column and a half out of what you have said now."

"Dear me! Can you really? Well, now, I should be careful, if I were you. I am afraid that, if you don't understand anything about art, you may give the public some very erroneous impressions."

"Oh, the public don't care a hang. All they want is to read something snappy and bright. That's what the public want. No, sir, we have catered too long for the public not to know what its size is. You might print the most learned article you could get hold of, it might be written by What's-his-name De Vinci, and be full of art slang, and all that sort of thing, but it wouldn't touch the general public at all."

"I don't suppose it would."

"What do you think of our Sunday papers here? You don't have any Sunday papers over in London."

"Oh yes, we do. But none of the big dailies have Sunday editions."

"They are not as big, or as enterprising as ours, are they? One Sunday paper, you know, prints about as much as two or three thirty-five cent magazines."

"What, the Sunday paper does?"

"Yes, the Sunday paper prints it, but doesn't sell for that. We give 'em more for the money than any magazine you ever saw."

"You certainly print some very large papers."

With this the reporter took his leave, and next morning Mr. Trenton saw the most astonishing account of his ideas on art matters imaginable. What struck him most forcibly was, that an article written by a person who admittedly knew nothing at all about art should be in general so free from error. The interview had a great number of head lines, and it was evident the paper desired to treat the artist with the utmost respect, and that it felt he showed his sense in preferring Boston to New York as a place of temporary residence; but what appalled him was the free and easy criticisms he was credited with having made on his own contemporaries in England. The principal points of each were summed up with a great deal of terseness and force, and in many cases were laughably true to life. It was evident that whoever touched up that interview possessed a very clear opinion and very accurate knowledge of the art movement in England.

Mr. Trenton thought he would sit down and write to the editor of the paper, correcting some of the more glaring inaccuracies; but a friend said -

"Oh, it is no use. Never mind. Nobody pays any attention to that. It's all right anyhow."

"Yes, but suppose the article should be copied in England, or suppose some of the papers should get over there?"

"Oh, that'll be all right," said his friend, with easy optimism. "Don't bother about it. They all know what a newspaper interview is; if they don't, why, you can tell them when you get back."

It was not long before Mr. Trenton found himself put down at all the principal clubs, both artistic and literary; and he also became, with a suddenness that bewildered him, quite the social lion for the time being. He was astonished to find that the receptions to which he was invited, and where he was, in a way, on exhibition, were really very grand occasions, and compared favourably with the finest gatherings he had had experience of in London.

His hostess at one of these receptions said to him, "Mr. Trenton, I want to introduce you to some of our art lovers in this city, whom I am sure you will be pleased to meet. I know that as a general thing the real artists are apt to despise the amateurs; but in this instance I hope you will be kind enough not to despise them, for my sake. We think they are really very clever indeed, and we like to be flattered by foreign preference."

"Am I the foreign preference in this instance?"

"You are, Mr. Trenton."

Robert Barr

"Now, I think it is too bad of you to say that, just when I have begun to feel as much at home in Boston as I do in London. I assure you I do not feel in the least foreign here. Neither do I maintain, like Mrs. Brown, that you are the foreigners."

"How very nice of you to say so, Mr. Trenton. Now I hope you will say something like that to the young lady I want you to meet. She is really very charming, and I am sure you will like her; and I may say, in parenthesis, that she, like the rest of us, is perfectly infatuated with your pictures."

As the lady said this, she brought Mr. Trenton in her wake, as it were, and said, "Miss Sommerton, allow me to present to you Mr. Trenton."

Miss Sommerton rose with graceful indolence, and held out her hand frankly to the artist. "Mr. Trenton," she said, "I am very pleased indeed to meet you. Have you been long in Boston?"

"Only a few days," replied Trenton. "I came up to Boston from Canada a short time since."

"Up? You mean down. We don't say up from Canada."

"Oh, don't you? Well, in England, you know, we say up to London, no matter from what part of the country we approach it. I think you are wrong in saying down, I think it really ought to be up to Boston from wherever you come."

His hostess appeared to be delighted with this bit of conversation, and she said, "I shall leave you two together for a few moments to get acquainted. Mr.

Trenton, you know you are in demand this evening."

"Do you think that is true?" said Trenton to Miss Sommerton.

"What?"

"Well, that I am in demand."

"I suppose it is true, if Mrs. Lennox says it is. You surely don't intend to cast any doubt on the word of your hostess, do you?"

"Oh, not at all. I didn't mean in a general way, you know, I meant in particular."

"I don't think I understand you, Mr. Trenton. By the way, you said you had been in Canada. Do you not think it is a very charming country?"

"Charming, Miss Sommerton, isn't the word for it. It is the most delightful country in the world."

"Ah, you say that because it belongs to England. I admit it is very delightful; but then there are other places on the Continent quite as beautiful as any part of Canada. You seem to have a prejudice in favour of monarchical institutions."

"Oh, is Canada monarchical? I didn't know that. I thought Canada was quite republican in its form of government."

"Well, it is a dependency; that's what I despise about Canada. Think of a glorious country like that, with hundreds of thousands of square miles, in fact, millions, I think, being dependent on a little island, away there among the fogs and rains, between the North Sea and the Atlantic Ocean. To be a dependency of some splendid tyrannical power like Russia wouldn't be so bad; but to be dependent on that little island - I lose all my respect for Canada when I think of it."

"Well, you know, the United States were colonies once."

"Ah, that is a very unfortunate comparison, Mr. Trenton. The moment the colonies, as you call them, came to years of discretion, they soon shook off their dependency. You must remember you are at Boston, and that the harbour is only a short distance from here."

"Does that mean that I should take advantage of its proximity and leave?"

"Oh, not at all. I could not say anything so rude, Mr. Trenton. Perhaps you are not familiar with the history of our trouble with England? Don't you remember it commenced in Boston Harbour practically?"

"Oh yes, I recollect now. I had forgotten it. Something about tea, was it not?"

"Yes, something about tea."

"Well, talking of tea, Miss Sommerton, may I take you to the conservatory and bring you a cup of it?"

"May I have an ice instead of the tea, if I prefer it, Mr, Trenton?"

"Why, certainly. You see how I am already dropping into the American phraseology."

"Oh, I think you are improving wonderfully, Mr. Trenton."

When they reached the conservatory, Miss Sommerton said -

"This is really a very great breach of good manners on both your part and mine. I have taken away the lion of the evening, and the lion has forgotten his duty to his hostess and to the other guests."

"Well, you see, I wanted to learn more of your ideas in the matter of dependencies. I don't at all agree with you on that. Now, I think if a country is conquered, it ought to be a dependency of the conquering people. It is the right of conquest. I - I am a thorough believer in the right of conquest."

"You seem to have very settled opinions on the matter, Mr. Trenton."

"I have indeed, Miss Sommerton. It is said that an Englishman never knows when he is conquered. Now I think that is a great mistake. There is no one so quick as an Englishman to admit that he has met his match."

"Why, have you met your match already, Mr. Trenton? Let me congratulate you."

"Well, don't congratulate me just yet. I am not at all certain whether I shall need any congratulations or not."

"I am sure I hope you will be very successful."

"Do you mean that?"

Miss Sommerton looked at him quietly for a moment.

"Do you think," she said, "I am in the habit of saying things I do not mean?"

"I think you are."

"Well, you are not a bit more complimentary than - than - you used to be."

"You were going to say than I was on the banks of the St. Maurice?"

"Oh, you visited the St. Maurice, did you? How far away from Boston that seems, doesn't it?"

"It is indeed a great distance, Miss Sommerton. But apparently not half as long as the round-about way we are traveling just now. Miss Sommerton, I waited and waited in Boston for you to return. I want to be a dependence. I admit the conquest. I wish to swear fealty to Miss Eva Sommerton of Boston, and now I ask my third question, will you accept the allegiance?"

Miss Sommerton was a little slow in replying, and before she had spoken Mrs. Lennox bustled in, and said -

"Oh, Mr. Trenton, I have been looking everywhere for you. There are a hundred people here who wish to be introduced, and all at once. May I have him, Miss Sommerton?"

"Well, Mrs. Lennox, you know, if I said 'Yes,' that would imply a certain ownership in him."

"I brought Miss Sommerton here to get her to accept an ice from me, which as yet I have not had the privilege of bringing. Will you accept - the ice, Miss Sommerton?"

The young lady blushed, as she looked at the artist.

"Yes," she said with a sigh; the tone was almost inaudible.

The artist hurried away to bring the refreshment.

"Why, Eva Sommerton," cried Mrs. Lennox, "you accept a plate of ice cream as tragically as if you were giving the answer to a proposal."

Mrs. Lennox said afterward that she thought there was something very peculiar about Miss Sommerton's smile in reply to her remark.

THE HERALDS OF FAME

CHAPTER I.

Now, when each man's place in literature is so clearly defined, it seems ridiculous to state that there was a time when Kenan Buel thought J. Lawless Hodden a great novelist. One would have imagined that Buel's keen insight into human nature would have made such a mistake impossible, but it must be remembered that Buel was always more or less of a hero-worshipper. It seems strange in the light of our after-knowledge that there ever was a day when Hodden's books were selling by the thousand, and Buel was tramping the streets of London fruitlessly searching for a publisher. Not less strange is the fact that Buel thought Hodden's success well deserved. He would have felt honoured by the touch of Hodden's hand.

No convict ever climbed a treadmill with more hopeless despair than Buel worked in his little room under the lofty roof. He knew no one; there were none to speak to him a cheering or comforting word; he was ignorant even of the names of the men who accepted the articles from his pen, which appeared unsigned in the daily papers and in some of the weeklies. He got cheques - small ones - with illegible and impersonal signatures that told him nothing. But the bits of paper were honoured at the bank, and this lucky fact enabled him to live and write books which publishers would not look at.

Nevertheless, showing how all things are possible to a desperate and resolute man, two of his books had already seen the light, if it could be called light. The first he was still paying for, on the instalment plan. The publishers were to pay half, and he was to pay half. This seemed to him only a fair division of the risk at the time. Not a single paper had paid the slightest attention to the book. The universal ignoring of it disheartened him. He had been prepared for abuse, but not for impenetrable silence.

He succeeded in getting another and more respectable publisher to take up his next book on a royalty arrangement. This was a surprise to him, and a gratification. His satisfaction did not last long after the book came out. It was mercilessly slated. One paper advised him to read "Hodden;" another said he had plagiarized from that popular writer. The criticisms cut him like a whip. He wondered why he had rebelled at the previous silence. He felt like a man who had heedlessly hurled a stone at a snow mountain and had been buried by the resulting avalanche.

He got his third publisher a year after that. He thought he would never succeed in getting the same firm twice, and wondered what would happen when he exhausted the London list. It is not right that a man should go on for ever without a word of encouragement. Fate recognised that there would come a breaking-point, and relented in time. The word came from an unexpected source. Buel was labouring, heavy-eyed, at the last proof-sheets of his third book, and was wondering whether he would have the courage not to look at the newspapers when the volume was published. He wished he could afford to go to some wilderness until the worst was over. He knew he could not miss the first notice, for experience had taught him that Snippit & Co., a clipping agency, would send it to him, with a nice type-written letter, saying -

"DEAR SIR,

"As your book is certain to attract a great deal of attention from the Press, we shall be pleased to send you clippings similar to the enclosed at the following rates."

It struck him as rather funny that any company should expect a sane man to pay so much good money for Press notices, mostly abusive. He never subscribed.

The word of encouragement gave notice of its approach in a letter, signed by a man of whom he had never heard. It was forwarded to him by his publishers. The letter ran: -

"DEAR SIR,

"Can you make it convenient to lunch with me on Friday at the Métropole? If you have an engagement for that day can you further oblige me by writing and putting it off? Tell the other fellow you are ill or have broken your leg, or anything, and charge up the fiction to me. I deal in fiction, anyhow. I leave on Saturday for the Continent, not wishing to spend another Sunday in London if I can avoid it. I have arranged to get out your book in America, having read the proof-sheets at your publisher's. All the business part of the transaction is settled, but I would like to see you personally if you don't mind, to have a talk over the future - always an interesting subject.

"Yours very truly,

"L. F. BRANT,

"Of Rainham Bros., Publishers, New York."

Buel read this letter over and over again. He had never seen anything exactly like it. There was a genial flippancy about it that was new to him, and he wondered what sort of a man the New Yorker was. Mr. Brant wrote to a stranger with the familiarity of an old friend, yet the letter warmed Buel's heart. He smiled at the idea the American evidently had about a previous engagement. Invitations to lunch become frequent when a man does not need them. No broken leg story would have to be told. He wrote and accepted Mr. Brant's invitation.

"You're Mr Buel, I think?"

The stranger's hand rested lightly on the young author's shoulder. Buel had just entered the unfamiliar precincts of the Métropole Hotel. The tall man with the gold lace on his hat had hesitated a moment before he swung open the big door, Buel was so evidently not a guest of the hotel.

"My name is Buel."

"Then you're my victim. I've been waiting impatiently for you. I am L. F. Brant."

"I thought I was in time. I am sorry to have kept

you waiting."

"Don't mention it. I have been waiting but thirty seconds. Come up in the elevator. They call it a lift here, not knowing any better, but it gets there ultimately, I have the title-deeds to a little parlour while I am staying in this tavern, and I thought we could talk better if we had lunch there. Lunch costs more on that basis, but I guess we can stand it."

A cold shudder passed over the thin frame of Kenan Buel. He did not know but it was the custom in America to ask a man to lunch and expect him to pay half. Brant's use of the plural lent colour to this view, and Buel knew he could not pay his share. He regretted they were not in a vegetarian restaurant.

The table in the centre of the room was already set for two, and the array of wine-glasses around each plate looked tempting. Brant pushed the electric button, drew up his chair, and said -

"Sit down, Buel, sit down. What's your favourite brand of wine? Let's settle on it now, so as to have no unseemly wrangle when the waiter comes. I'm rather in awe of the waiter. It doesn't seem natural that any mere human man should be so obviously superior to the rest of us mortals as this waiter is. I'm going to give you only the choice of the first wines. I have taken the champagne for granted, and it's cooling now in a tub somewhere. We always drink champagne in the States, not because we like it, but because it's expensive. I calculate that I pay the expenses of my trip over here merely by ordering unlimited champagne. I save more than a dollar a bottle on New York prices, and these saved dollars count up in a month. Personally I prefer cider or lager beer, but in New York we dare not own to liking a thing unless it is expensive."

"It can hardly be a pleasant place for a poor man to live in, if that is the case."

"My dear Buel, no city is a pleasant place for a poor man to live in. I don't suppose New York is worse than London in that respect. The poor have a hard time of it anywhere. A man owes it to himself and family not to be poor. Now, that's one thing I like about your book; you touch on poverty in a sympathetic way, by George, like a man who had come through it himself. I've been there, and I know how it is. When I first struck New York I hadn't even a ragged dollar bill to my back. Of course every successful man will tell you the same of himself, but it is mostly brag, and in half the instances it isn't true at all; but in my case - well, I wasn't subscribing to the heathen in those days. I made up my mind that poverty didn't pay, and I have succeeded in remedying the state of affairs. But I haven't forgotten how it felt to be hard up, and I sympathise with those who are. Nothing would afford me greater pleasure than to give a helping hand to a fellow - that is, to a clever fellow who was worth saving - who is down at bed rock. Don't you feel that way too?"

"Yes," said Buel, with some hesitation, "it would be a pleasure."

"I knew when I read your book you felt that way - I was sure of it. Well, I've helped a few in my time; but I regret to say most of them turned out to be no good. That is where the trouble is. Those who are really deserving are just the persons who die of starvation in a garret, and never let the outside world know their trouble."

"I do not doubt such is often the case."

"Of course it is. It's always the case. But here's the soup. I hope you have brought a good appetite. You can't expect such a meal here as you would get in New York; but they do fairly well. I, for one, don't grumble about the food in London, as most Americans do. Londoners manage to keep alive, and that, after all, is the main thing."

Buel was perfectly satisfied with the meal, and thought if they produced a better one in New York, or anywhere else, the art of cookery had reached wonderful perfection. Brant, however, kept apologising for the spread as he went along. The talk drifted on in an apparently aimless fashion, but the publisher was a shrewd man, and he was gradually leading it up to the point he had in view from the beginning, and all the while he was taking the measure of his guest. He was not a man to waste either his time or his dinners without an object. When he had once "sized up" his man, as he termed it, he was either exceedingly frank and open with him, or the exact opposite, as suited his purpose. He told Buel that he came to England once a year, if possible, rapidly scanned the works of fiction about to be published by the various houses in London, and made arrangements for the producing of those in America that he thought would go down with the American people.

"I suppose," said Buel, "that you have met many of the noted authors of this country?"

"All of them, I think; all of them, at one time or

another. The publishing business has its drawbacks like every other trade," replied Brant, jauntily.

"Have you met Hodden?"

"Several times. Conceited ass!"

"You astonish me. I have never had the good fortune to become acquainted with any of our celebrated writers. I would think it a privilege to know Hodden and some of the others."

"You're lucky, and you evidently don't know it. I would rather meet a duke any day than a famous author. The duke puts on less side and patronises you less."

"I would rather be a celebrated author than a duke if I had my choice."

"Well, being a free and independent citizen of the Democratic United States, I wouldn't. *No*, sir! I would rather be Duke Brant any day in the week than Mr. Brant, the talented author of, etc., etc. The moment an author receives a little praise and becomes talked about, he gets what we call in the States 'the swelled head.' I've seen some of the nicest fellows in the world become utterly spoiled by a little success. And then think of the absurdity of it all. There aren't more than two or three at the most of the present-day writers who will be heard of a century hence. Read the history of literature, and you will find that never more than four men in any one generation are heard of after. Four is a liberal allowance. What has any writer to be conceited about anyhow? Let him read his Shakespeare and be modest."

Buel said with a sigh, "I wish there was success in store for me. I would risk the malady you call the 'swelled head.'"

"Success will come all right enough, my boy. 'All things come to him who waits,' and while he is waiting puts in some good, strong days of work. It's the working that tells, not the waiting. And now, if you will light one of these cigars, we will talk of you for a while, if your modesty will stand it. What kind of Chartreuse will you have? Yellow or green?"

"Either."

"Take the green, then. Where the price is the same I always take the green. It is the stronger, and you get more for your money. Now then, I will be perfectly frank with you. I read your book in the proof-sheets, and I ran it down in great style to your publisher."

"I am sorry you did not like it."

"I don't say I didn't like it. I ran it down because it was business. I made up my mind when I read that book to give a hundred pounds for the American rights. I got it for twenty."

Brant laughed, and Buel felt uncomfortable. He feared that after all he did not like this frank American.

"Having settled about the book, I wanted to see you, and here you are. Of course, I am utterly selfish in wanting to see you, for I wish you to promise me that we will have the right of publishing your books in America as long as we pay as much as any other publisher. There is nothing unfair in that, is there?"

"No. I may warn you, however, that there has been no great competition, so far, for the privilege of doing any publishing, either here or in America."

"That's all right. Unless I'm a Dutchman there will be, after your new book is published. Of course, that is one of the things no fellow can find out. If he could, publishing would be less of a lottery than it is. A book is sometimes a success by the merest fluke; at other times, in spite of everything, a good book is a deplorable failure. I think yours will go; anyhow, I am willing to bet on it up to a certain amount, and if it does go, I want to have the first look-in at your future books. What do you say?"

"Do you wish me to sign a contract?"

"No, I merely want your word. You may write me a letter if you like, that I could show to my partners, saying that we would have the first refusal of your future books."

"I am quite willing to do that."

"Very good. That's settled. Now, you look fagged out. I wish you would take a trip over to New York. I'll look after you when you get there. It would do you a world of good, and would show in the pages of your next book. What do you say to that? Have you any engagements that would prevent you making the trip?"

Buel laughed, "I am perfectly free as far as engagements are concerned."

"That's all right, then. I wish I were in that position. Now, as I said, I considered your book cheap at £100. I got it for £20. I propose to hand over the £80 to you. I'll write out the cheque as soon as the waiters clear away the *débris*. Then your letter to the firm would form the receipt for this money, and - well, it need not be a contract, you know, or anything formal, but just your ideas on any future business that may crop up."

"I must say I think your offer is very generous."

"Oh, not at all. It is merely business. The £80 is on account of royalties. If the book goes, as I think it will, I hope to pay you much more than that. Now I hope you will come over and see me as soon as you can."

"Yes. As you say, the trip will do me good. I have been rather hard at it for some time."

"Then I'll look out for you. I sail on the French line Saturday week. When will you come?"

"As soon as my book is out here, and before any of the reviews appear."

"Sensible man. What's your cable address?"

"I haven't one."

"Well, I suppose a telegram to your publishers will find you. I'll cable if anything turns up unexpectedly. You send me over a despatch saying what steamer you sail on. My address is 'Rushing, New York.' Just cable the name of the steamer, and I will be on the look-out for you."

It was doubtless the effect of the champagne, for Buel went back to his squalid room with his mind in the clouds. He wondered if this condition was the first indication of the swelled head Brant had talked about. Buel worked harder than ever at his proofs, and there was some growling at head-quarters because of the numerous corrections he made. These changes were regarded as impudence on the part of so unknown a man. He sent off to America a set of the corrected proofs, and received a cablegram, "Proofs received. Too late. Book published today."

This was a disappointment. Still he had the consolation of knowing that the English edition would be as perfect as he could make it. He secured a berth on the *Geranium*, sailing from Liverpool, and cabled Brant to that effect. The day before he sailed he got a cablegram that bewildered him. It was simply, "She's a-booming." He regretted that he had never learned the American language.

CHAPTER II.

Kenan Buel received from his London publisher a brown paper parcel, and on opening it found the contents to be six exceedingly new copies of his book. Whatever the publisher thought of the inside of the work, he had not spared pains to make the outside as attractive as it could be made at the price. Buel turned it over and over, and could almost imagine himself buying a book that looked so tastefully got up as this one. The sight of the volume gave him a thrill, for he remembered that the Press doubtless received its quota at about the same time his parcel came, and he feared he would not be out of the country before the first extract from the clipping agency arrived. However, luck was with the young man, and he found himself on the platform of Euston Station, waiting for the Liverpool express, without having seen anything about his book in the papers, except a brief line giving its title, the price, and his own name, in the "Books Received" column.

As he lingered around the well-kept bookstall before the train left, he saw a long row of Hodden's new novel, and then his heart gave a jump as he caught sight of two copies of his own work in the row labelled "New Books." He wanted to ask the clerk whether any of them had been sold yet, but in the first place he lacked the courage, and in the second place the clerk was very busy. As he stood there, a comely young woman, equipped for traveling, approached the stall, and ran her eye hurriedly up and down the tempting array of literature. She bought several of the illustrated papers, and then scanned the new books. The clerk, following her eye, picked out Buel's book.

"Just out, miss. Three and sixpence."

"Who is the author?" asked the girl.

"Kenan Buel, a new man," answered the clerk, without a moment's hesitation, and without looking at the title-page. "Very clever work."

Buel was astonished at the knowledge shown by the clerk. He knew that W.H. Smith & Son never had a book of his before, and he wondered how the clerk apparently knew so much of the volume and its author, forgetting that it was the clerk's business. The girl listlessly ran the leaves of the book past the edge of her thumb. It seemed to Buel that the fate of the whole edition was in her hands, and he watched her breathlessly, even forgetting how charming she looked. There stood the merchant eager to sell, and there, in the form of a young woman, was the great public. If she did not buy, why should any one else; and if nobody bought, what chance had an unknown author?

She put the book down, and looked up as she heard some one sigh deeply near her.

"Have you Hodden's new book?" she asked.

"Yes, miss. Six shillings."

The clerk quickly put Buel's book beside its lone companion, and took down Hodden's.

"Thank you," said the girl, giving him a half sovereign; and, taking the change, she departed with her bundle of literature to the train.

Buel said afterwards that what hurt him most in this painful incident was the fact that if it were repeated often the bookstall clerk would lose faith in the book. He had done so well for a man who could not possibly have read a word of the volume, that Buel felt sorry on the clerk's account rather than his own that the copy had not been sold. He walked to the end of the platform, and then back to the bookstall.

"Has that new book of Buel's come out yet?" he asked the clerk in an unconcerned tone.

"Yes, sir. Here it is; three and sixpence, sir."

"Thank you," said Buel, putting his hand in his pocket for the money. "How is it selling?"

"Well, sir, there won't be much call for it, not likely, till the reviews begin to come out."

There, Mr. Buel, you had a lesson, if you had only taken it to heart, or pondered on its meaning. Since then you have often been very scornful of newspaper reviews, yet you saw yourself how the great public treats a man who is not even abused. How were you to know that the column of grossly unfair rancour which *The Daily Argus* poured out on your book two days later, when you were sailing serenely over the Atlantic, would make that same clerk send in four separate orders to the "House" during the week? Medicine may have a bad taste, and yet have beneficial results. So Mr. Kenan Buel, after buying a book of which he had six copies in his portmanteau, with no one to give them to, took his place in the train, and in due time found himself at Liverpool and on board the *Geranium*.

The stewards being busy, Buel placed his portmanteau on the deck, and, with his newly bought volume in his hand, the string and brown paper still around it, he walked up and down on the empty side of the deck, noticing how scrupulously clean the ship was. It was the first time he had ever been on board a steamship, and he could not trust himself unguided to explore the depths below, and see what kind of a state-room and what sort of a companion chance had allotted to him. They had told him when he bought his ticket that the steamer would be very crowded that trip, so many Americans were returning; but his state-room had berths for only two, and he had a faint hope the other fellow would not turn up. As he paced the deck his thoughts wandered to the pretty girl who did not buy his book. He had seen her again on the tender in company with a serene and placid older woman, who sat unconcernedly, surrounded by bundles, shawls, straps, valises, and hand-bags, which the girl nervously counted every now and then, fruitlessly trying to convince the elderly lady that something must have been left behind in the train, or lost in transit from the station to the steamer. The worry of travel, which the elderly woman absolutely refused to share, seemed to rest with double weight on the shoulders of the girl.

As Buel thought of all this, he saw the girl approach him along the deck with a smile of apparent recognition on her face. "She evidently mistakes me for some one else," he said to himself. "Oh, thank you," she cried, coming near, and holding out her hand. "I see you have found my book."

He helplessly held out the package to her, which she took.

"Is it yours?" he asked.

"Yes, I recognised it by the string. I bought it at Euston Station. I am forever losing things," she added. "Thank you, ever so much."

Buel laughed to himself as she disappeared. "Fate evidently intends her to read my book," he said to himself. "She will think the clerk has made a mistake. I must get her unbiased opinion of it before the voyage ends."

The voyage at that moment was just beginning, and the thud, thud of the screw brought that fact to his knowledge. He sought a steward, and asked him to carry the portmanteau to berth 159.

"You don't happen to know whether there is any one else in that room or not, do you?" he asked.

"It's likely there is, sir. The ship's very full this voyage."

Buel followed him into the saloon, and along the seemingly interminable passage; then down a narrow side alley, into which a door opened marked 159-160. The steward rapped at the door, and, as there was no response, opened it. All hopes of a room to himself vanished as Buel looked into the small state-room.

There was a steamer trunk on the floor, a portmanteau on the seat, while the two bunks were covered with a miscellaneous assortment of hand-bags, shawl-strap bundles, and packages.

The steward smiled. "I think he wants a room to himself," he said.

On the trunk Buel noticed the name in white letters "Hodden," and instantly there arose within him a hope that his companion was to be the celebrated novelist. This hope was strengthened when he saw on the portmanteau the letters "J.L.H.," which were the novelist's initials. He pictured to himself interesting conversations on the way over, and hoped he would receive some particulars from the novelist's own lips of his early struggles for fame. Still, he did not allow himself to build too much on his supposition, for there are a great many people in this world, and the chances were that the traveller would be some commonplace individual of the same name.

The steward placed Buel's portmanteau beside the other, and backed out of the overflowing cabin. All doubt as to the identity of the other occupant was put at rest by the appearance down the passage of a man whom Buel instantly recognised by the portraits he had seen of him in the illustrated papers. He was older than the pictures made him appear, and there was a certain querulous expression on his face which was also absent in the portraits. He glanced into the state-room, looked for a moment through Buel, and then turned to the steward.

"What do you mean by putting that portmanteau into my room?"

"This gentleman has the upper berth, sir."

"Nonsense. The entire room is mine. Take the portmanteau out."

The steward hesitated, looking from one to the other.

"The ticket is for 159, sir," he said at last.

"Then there is some mistake. The room is mine. Don't have me ask you again to remove the portmanteau."

"Perhaps you would like to see the purser, sir."

"I have nothing to do with the purser. Do as I tell you."

All this time he had utterly ignored Buel, whose colour was rising. The young man said quietly to the steward, "Take out the portmanteau, please."

When it was placed in the passage, Hodden entered the room, shut and bolted the door.

"Will you see the purser, sir?" said the steward in an awed whisper.

"I think so. There is doubtless some mistake, as he says."

The purser was busy allotting seats at the tables, and Buel waited patiently. He had no friends on board, and did not care where he was placed.

When the purser was at liberty, the steward explained to him the difficulty which had arisen. The official looked at his list.

"159 - Buel. Is that your name, sir? Very good; 160 - Hodden. That is the gentleman now in the room. Well, what is the trouble?"

"Mr Hodden says, sir, that the room belongs to him."

"Have you seen his ticket?"

"No, sir."

"Then bring it to me."

"Mistakes sometimes happen, Mr. Buel," said the purser, when the steward vanished. "But as a general thing I find that people simply claim what they have no right to claim. Often the agents promise that if possible a passenger shall have a room to himself, and when we can do so we let him have it. I try to please everybody; but all the steamers crossing to America are full at this season of the year, and it is not practicable to give every one the whole ship to himself. As the Americans say, some people want the earth for £12 or £15, and we can't always give it to them. Ah, here is the ticket. It is just as I thought. Mr. Hodden is entitled merely to berth 160."

The arrival of the ticket was quickly followed by the advent of Mr. Hodden himself. He still ignored Buel.

"Your people in London," he said to the purser, "guaranteed me a room to myself. Otherwise I would not have come on this line. Now it seems that another person has been put in with me. I must protest against this kind of usage."

"Have you any letter from them guaranteeing the

room?" asked the purser blandly.

"No. I supposed until now that their word was sufficient."

"Well, you see, I am helpless in this case. These two tickets are exactly the same with the exception of the numbers. Mr. Buel has just as much right to insist on being alone in the room as far as the tickets go, and I have had no instructions in the matter."

"But it is an outrage that they should promise me one thing in London, and then refuse to perform it, when I am helpless on the ocean."

"If they have done so -"

"*If* they have done so? Do you doubt my word, sir?"

"Oh, not at all, sir, not at all," answered the purser in his most conciliatory tone. "But in that case your ticket should have been marked 159-160."

"I am not to suffer for their blunders."

"I see by this list that you paid £12 for your ticket. Am I right?"

"That was the amount, I believe. I paid what I was asked to pay."

"Quite so, sir. Well, you see, that is the price of one berth only. Mr. Buel, here, paid the same amount."

"Come to the point. Do I understand you to refuse to remedy the mistake (to put the matter in its mildest form) of your London people?"

"I do not refuse. I would be only too glad to give you the room to yourself, if it were possible. Unfortunately, it is not possible. I assure you there is not an unoccupied state-room on the ship."

"Then I will see the captain. Where shall I find him?"

"Very good, sir. Steward, take Mr. Hodden to the captain's room."

When they were alone again Buel very contritely expressed his sorrow at having been the innocent cause of so much trouble to the purser.

"Bless you, sir, I don't mind it in the least. This is a very simple case. Where both occupants of a room claim it all to themselves, and where both are angry and abuse me at the same time, then it gets a bit lively. I don't envy him his talk with the captain. If the old man happens to be feeling a little grumpy today, and he most generally does at the beginning of the voyage, Mr. Hodden will have a bad ten minutes. Don't you bother a bit about it, sir, but go down to your room and make yourself at home. It will be all right."

Mr. Hodden quickly found that the appeal to Caesar was not well timed. The captain had not the suave politeness of the purser. There may be greater and more powerful men on earth than the captain of an ocean liner, but you can't get any seafaring man to believe it, and the captains themselves are rarely without a due sense of their own dignity. The man who tries to bluff the captain of a steamship like the *Geranium* has a hard row to hoe. Mr. Hodden descended to his state-room in a more subdued frame of mind than when he went on the upper deck. However, he still felt able to crush his unfortunate room-mate.

"You insist, then," he said, speaking to Buel for the first time, "on occupying this room?"

"I have no choice in the matter."

"I thought perhaps you might feel some hesitation in forcing yourself in where you were so evidently not wanted?"

The hero-worshipper in Buel withered, and the natural Englishman asserted itself.

"I have exactly the same right in this room that you have. I claim no privilege which I have not paid for."

"Do you wish to suggest that I have made such a claim?"

"I suggest nothing; I state it. You *have* made such a claim, and in a most offensive manner."

"Do you understand the meaning of the language you are using, sir? You are calling me a liar."

"You put it very tersely, Mr. Hodden. Thank you. Now, if you venture to address me again during this voyage, I shall be obliged if you keep a civil tongue in your head."

"Good heavens! *You* talk of civility?" cried the astonished man, aghast.

His room-mate went to the upper deck. In the next state-room pretty Miss Carrie Jessop clapped her small hands silently together. The construction of staterooms is such that every word uttered in one above the breath is audible in the next room; Miss Jessop could not help hearing the whole controversy, from the time the steward was ordered so curtly to remove the portmanteau, until the culmination of the discussion and the evident defeat of Mr. Hodden. Her sympathy was all with the other fellow, at that moment unknown, but a sly peep past the edge of the scarcely opened door told her that the unnamed party in the quarrel was the awkward young man who had found her book. She wondered if the Hodden mentioned could possibly be the author, and, with a woman's inconsistency, felt sure that she would detest the story, as if the personality of the writer had anything whatever to do with his work. She took down the parcel from the shelf and undid the string. Her eyes opened wide as she looked at the title.

"Well I never!" she gasped. "If I haven't robbed that poor, innocent young man of a book he bought for himself! Attempted eviction by his room-mate, and bold highway robbery by an unknown woman! No, it's worse than that; it's piracy, for it happened on the high seas." And the girl laughed softly to herself.

CHAPTER III.

Kenan Buel walked the deck alone in the evening light, and felt that he ought to be enjoying the calmness and serenity of the ocean expanse around him after the noise and squalor of London; but now that the excitement of the recent quarrel was over, he felt the reaction, and his natural diffidence led him to blame himself. Most of the passengers were below, preparing for dinner, and he had the deck to himself. As he turned on one of his rounds, he saw approaching him the girl of Euston Station, as he mentally termed her. She had his book in her hand.

"I have come to beg your pardon," she said. "I see it was your own book I took from you to day."

"My own book!" cried Buel, fearing she had somehow discovered his guilty secret. "Yes. Didn't you buy this for yourself?" She held up the volume.

"Oh, certainly. But you are quite welcome to it, I am sure."

"I couldn't think of taking it away from you before you have read it."

"But I have read it," replied Buel, eagerly: "and I shall be very pleased to lend it to you."

"Indeed? And how did you manage to read it without undoing the parcel?"

"That is to say I - I skimmed over it before it was done up," he said in confusion. The clear eyes of the girl disconcerted him, and, whatever his place in fiction is now, he was at that time a most unskilful liar.

"You see, I bought it because it is written by a namesake of mine. My name is Buel, and I happened to notice that was the name on the book; in fact, if you remember, when you were looking over it at the stall, the clerk mentioned the author's name, and that naturally caught my attention."

The girl glanced with renewed interest at the volume.

"Was this the book I was looking at? The story I bought was Hodden's latest. I found it a moment ago down in my state-room, so it was not lost after all."

They were now walking together as if they were old acquaintances, the girl still holding the volume in her hand.

"By the way," she said innocently, "I see on the passenger list that there is a Mr. Hodden on board. Do you think he can be the novelist?"

"I believe he is," answered Buel, stiffly.

"Oh, that will be too jolly for anything. I would *so* like to meet him. I am sure he must be a most charming man. His books show such insight into human nature, such sympathy and noble purpose. There could be nothing petty or mean about such a man."

"I - I - suppose not."

"Why, of course there couldn't. You have read his books, have you not?"

"All of them except his latest."

"Well, I'll lend you that, as you have been so kind as to offer me the reading of this one."

"Thank you. After you have read it yourself."

"And when you have become acquainted with Mr. Hodden, I want you to introduce him to me."

"With pleasure. And - and when I do so, who shall I tell him the young lady is?"

The audacious girl laughed lightly, and, stepping back, made him a saucy bow.

"You will introduce me as Miss Caroline Jessop, of New York. Be sure that you say 'New York,' for that will account to Mr. Hodden for any eccentricities of conduct or conversation he may be good enough to notice. I suppose you think American girls are very forward? All Englishmen do."

"On the contrary, I have always understood that they are very charming."

"Indeed? And so you are going over to see?"

Buel laughed. All the depression he felt a short time before had vanished.

"I had no such intention when I began the voyage, but even if I should quit the steamer at Queenstown, I could bear personal testimony to the truth of the statement."

"Oh, Mr. Buel, that is very nicely put. I don't think you can improve on it, so I shall run down and dress for dinner. There is the first gong. Thanks for the book."

The young man said to himself, "Buel, my boy, you're getting on;" and he smiled as he leaned over the bulwark and looked at the rushing water. He sobered instantly as he remembered that he would have to go to his state-room and perhaps meet Hodden. It is an awkward thing to quarrel with your room-mate at the beginning of a long voyage. He hoped Hodden had taken his departure to the saloon, and he lingered until the second gong rang. Entering the stateroom, he found Hodden still there. Buel gave him no greeting. The other cleared his throat several times and then said -

"I have not the pleasure of knowing your name."

"My name is Buel."

"Well, Mr. Buel, I am sorry that I spoke to you in the manner I did, and I hope you will allow me to apologise for doing so. Various little matters had combined to irritate me, and - Of course, that is no excuse. But -"

"Don't say anything more. I unreservedly retract what I was heated enough to say, and so we may consider the episode ended. I may add that if the purser has a vacant berth anywhere, I shall be very glad to take it, if the occupants of the room make no objection."

"You are very kind," said Hodden, but he did not make any show of declining the offer.

"Very well, then, let us settle the matter while we are at it." And Buel pressed the electric button.

The steward looked in, saying, -

"Dinner is ready, gentlemen."

"Yes, I know. Just ask the purser if he can step here for a moment."

The purser came promptly, and if he was disturbed at being called at such a moment he did not show it. Pursers are very diplomatic persons.

"Have you a vacant berth anywhere, purser?"

An expression faintly suggestive of annoyance passed over the purser's serene brow. He thought the matter had been settled. "We have several berths vacant, but they are each in rooms that already contain three persons."

"One of those will do for me; that is, if the occupants have no objection."

"It will be rather crowded, sir."

"That doesn't matter, if the others are willing."

"Very good, sir. I will see to it immediately after dinner."

The purser was as good as his word, and introduced

Buel and his portmanteau to a room that contained three wild American collegians who had been doing Europe "on the cheap" and on foot. They received the new-comer with a hilariousness that disconcerted him.

"Hello, purser!" cried one, "this is an Englishman. You didn't tell us you were going to run in an Englishman on us."

"Never, mind, we'll convert him on the way over."

"I say, purser, if you sling a hammock from the ceiling and put up a cot on the floor you can put two more men in here. Why didn't you think of that?"

"It's not too late yet. Why did you suggest it?"

"Gentlemen," said Buel, "I have no desire to intrude, if it is against your wish."

"Oh, that's all right. Never mind them. They have to talk or die. The truth is, we were lonesome without a fourth man."

"What's his name, purser?"

"My name is Buel."

One of them shouted out the inquiry, "What's the matter with Buel?" and all answered in concert with a yell that made the steamer ring, "*He's* all right."

"You'll have to sing 'Hail Columbia' night and morning if you stay in this cabin."

"Very good," said Buel, entering into the spirit of the

occasion. "Singing is not my strong point, and after you hear me at it once, you will be glad to pay a heavy premium to have it stopped."

"Say, Buel, can you play poker?"

"No, but I can learn."

"That's business. America's just yearning for men who can learn. We have had so many Englishmen who know it all, that we'll welcome a change. But poker's an expensive game to acquire."

"Don't be bluffed, Mr. Buel. Not one of the crowd has enough money left to buy the drinks all round. We would never have got home if we hadn't return tickets."

"Say, boys, let's lock the purser out, and make Buel an American citizen before he can call for help. You solemnly swear that you hereby and hereon renounce all emperors, kings, princes, and potentates, and more especially - how does the rest of it go!"

"He must give up his titles, honours, knighthoods, and things of that sort."

"Say, Buel, you're not a lord or a duke by any chance? Because, if you are, we'll call back the purser and have you put out yet."

"No, I haven't even the title esquire, which, I under-stand, all American citizens possess."

"Oh, you'll do. Now, I propose that Mr. Buel take his choice of the four bunks, and that we raffle for the rest."

When Buel reached the deck out of this pandemonium, he looked around for another citizen of the United States, but she was not there. He wondered if she were reading his book, and how she liked it.

CHAPTER IV.

Next morning Mr. Buel again searched the deck for the fair American, and this time he found her reading his book, seated very comfortably in her deck chair. The fact that she was so engaged put out of Buel's mind the greeting he had carefully prepared beforehand, and he stood there awkwardly, not knowing what to say. He inwardly cursed his unreadiness, and felt, to his further embarrassment, that his colour was rising. He was not put more at his ease when Miss Jessop looked up at him coldly, with a distinct frown on her pretty face.

"Mr. Buel, I believe?" she said pertly.

"I - I think so," he stammered.

She went on with her reading, ignoring him, and he stood there not knowing how to get away. When he pulled himself together, after a few moments' silence, and was about to depart, wondering at the caprice of womankind, she looked up again, and said icily -

"Why don't you ask me to walk with you? Do you think you have no duties, merely because you are on shipboard?"

"It isn't a duty, it is a pleasure, if you will come with me. I was afraid I had offended you in some way."

"You have. That is why I want to walk with you. I wish to give you a piece of my mind, and it won't be pleasant to listen to, I can assure you. So there must be no listener but yourself."

"Is it so serious as that?"

"Quite. Assist me, please. Why do you have to be asked to do such a thing? I don't suppose there is another man on the ship who would see a lady struggling with her rugs, and never put out his hand."

Before the astonished young man could offer assistance the girl sprang to her feet and stood beside him. Although she tried to retain her severe look of displeasure, there was a merry twinkle in the corner of her eye, as if she enjoyed shocking him.

"I fear I am very unready."

"You are."

"Will you take my arm as we walk?"

"Certainly not," she answered, putting the tips of her fingers into the shallow pockets of her pilot jacket. "Don't you know the United States are long since independent of England?"

"I had forgotten for the moment. My knowledge of history is rather limited, even when I try to remember. Still, independence and all, the two countries may be friends, may they not?"

"I doubt it. It seems to be natural that an American should hate an Englishman."

"Dear me, is it so bad as that? Why, may I ask? Is it on account of the little trouble in 1770, or whenever it was?"

"1776, when we conquered you."

"Were we conquered? That is another historical fact which has been concealed from me. I am afraid England doesn't quite realise her unfortunate position. She has a good deal of go about her for a conquered nation. But I thought the conquering, which we all admit, was of much more recent date, when the pretty American girls began to come over. Then Englishmen, at once capitulated."

"Yes," she cried scornfully. "And I don't know which to despise most, the American girls who marry Englishmen, or the Englishmen they marry. They are married for their money."

"Who? The Englishmen?"

The girl stamped her foot on the deck as they turned around.

"You know very well what I mean. An Englishman thinks of nothing but money."

"Really? I wonder where you got all your cut-and-dried notions about Englishmen? You seem to have a great capacity for contempt. I don't think it is good. My experience is rather limited, of course, but, as far as it goes, I find good and bad in all nations. There are Englishmen whom I find it impossible to like, and there are Americans whom I find I admire in spite of myself. There are also, doubtless, good Englishmen and bad Americans, if we only knew where to find them. You cannot sum up a nation and condemn it in a phrase, you know."

"Can't you? Well, literary Englishmen have tried to do so in the case of America. No English writer has ever dealt even fairly with the United States."

"Don't you think the States are a little too sensitive about the matter?"

"Sensitive? Bless you, we don't mind it a bit."

"Then where's the harm? Besides, America has its revenge in you. Your scathing contempt more than balances the account."

"I only wish I could write. Then I would let you know what I think of you."

"Oh, don't publish a book about us. I wouldn't like to see war between the two countries."

Miss Jessop laughed merrily for so belligerent a person.

"War?" she cried. "I hope yet to see an American army camped in London."

"If that is your desire, you can see it any day in summer. You will find them tenting out at the Métropole and all the expensive hotels. I bivouacked with an invader there some weeks ago, and he was enduring the rigours of camp life with great fortitude, mitigating his trials with unlimited champagne."

"Why, Mr. Buel," cried the girl admiringly, "you're beginning to talk just like an American yourself."

"Oh, now, you are trying to make me conceited."

Miss Jessop sighed, and shook her head.

"I had nearly forgotten," she said, "that I despised you. I remember now why I began to walk with you. It was not to talk frivolously, but to show you the depth of my contempt! Since yesterday you have gone down in my estimation from 190 to 56."

"Fahrenheit?"

"No, that was a Wall Street quotation. Your stock has 'slumped,' as we say on the Street."

"Now you are talking Latin, or worse, for I can understand a little Latin."

"'Slumped' sounds slangy, doesn't it? It isn't a pretty word, but it is expressive. It means going down with a run, or rather, all in a heap."

"What have I done?"

"Nothing you can say will undo it, so there is no use in speaking any more about it. Second thoughts are best. My second thought is to say no more."

"I must know my crime. Give me a chance to, at least, reach par again, even if I can't hope to attain the 90 above."

"I thought an Englishman had some grit. I thought he

did not allow any one to walk over him. I thought he stood by his guns when he knew he was in the right. I thought he was a manly man, and a fighter against injustice!"

"Dear me! Judging by your conversation of a few minutes ago, one would imagine that you attributed exactly the opposite qualities to him."

"I say I thought all this - yesterday. I don't think so to-day."

"Oh, I see! And all on account of me?"

"All on account of you."

"Once more, what have I done?"

"What have you done? You have allowed that detestably selfish specimen of your race, Hodden, to evict you from your room."

The young man stopped abruptly in his walk, and looked at the girl with astonishment. She, her hands still coquettishly thrust in her jacket-pockets, returned his gaze with unruffled serenity.

"What do you know about it?" he demanded at last.

"Everything. From the time you meekly told the steward to take out your valise until the time you meekly apologised to Hodden for having told him the truth, and then meekly followed the purser to a room containing three others."

"But Hodden meekly, as you express it, apologised

first. I suppose you know that too, otherwise I would not have mentioned it."

"Certainly he did. That was because he found his overbearing tactics did not work. He apologised merely to get rid of you, and did. That's what put me out of patience with you. To think, you couldn't see through his scheme!"

"Oh! I thought it was the lack of manly qualities you despised in me. Now you are accusing me of not being crafty."

"How severely you say that! You quite frighten me! You will be making me apologise by-and-by, and I don't want to do that."

Buel laughed, and resumed his walk.

"It's all right," he said; "Hodden's loss is my gain. I've got in with a jolly lot, who took the trouble last night to teach me the great American game at cards - and counters."

Miss Jessop sighed.

"Having escaped with my life," she said, "I think I shall not run any more risks, but shall continue with your book. I had no idea you could look so fierce. I have scarcely gotten over it yet. Besides, I am very much interested in that book of yours."

"Why do you say so persistently 'that book of mine'?"

"Isn't it yours? You bought it, didn't you? Then it was written by your relative, you know."

"I said my namesake."

"So you did. And now I'm going to ask you an impudent question. You will not look wicked again, will you?"

"I won't promise. That depends entirely on the question."

"It is easily answered."

"I'm waiting."

"What is your Christian name, Mr. Buel?"

"My Christian name?" he repeated, uncomfortably.

"Yes, what is it?"

"Why do you wish to know?"

"A woman's reason - because."

They walked the length of the deck in silence.

"Come, now," she said, "confess. What is it?"

"John."

Miss Jessop laughed heartily, but quietly.

"You think John commonplace, I suppose?"

"Oh, it suits *you*, Mr. Buel. Goodbye."

As the young woman found her place in the book, she

mused, "How blind men are, after all - with his name in full on the passage list." Then she said to herself, with a sigh, "I do wish I had bought this book instead of Hodden's."

CHAPTER V.

At first Mr. Hodden held somewhat aloof from his fellow-passengers; but, finding perhaps that there was no general desire to intrude upon him, he condescended to become genial to a select few. He walked the deck alone, picturesquely attired. He was a man who paid considerable attention to his personal appearance. As day followed day, Mr. Hodden unbent so far as to talk frequently with Miss Jessop on what might almost be called equal terms. The somewhat startling opinions and unexpected remarks of the American girl appeared to interest him, and doubtless tended to confirm his previous unfavourable impressions of the inhabitants of the Western world. Mr. Buel was usually present during these conferences, and his conduct under the circumstances was not admirable. He was silent and moody, and almost gruff on some occasions. Perhaps Hodden's persistent ignoring of him, and the elder man's air of conscious superiority, irritated Buel; but if he had had the advantage of mixing much in the society of his native land he would have become accustomed to that. People thrive on the condescension of the great; they like it, and boast about it. Yet Buel did not seem to be pleased. But the most astounding thing was that the young man should actually have taken it upon himself to lecture Miss Jessop once, when they were alone, for some remarks she had made to Hodden as she sat in her deck-chair, with Hodden loquacious on her right and Buel taciturn on her left. What right had Buel to find fault with a free and independent citizen of another country? Evidently none. It might have been expected that Miss Jessop, rising to the occasion, would have taught the young man his place, and would perhaps have made some scathing remark about the tendency of Englishmen to interfere in matters that did not concern them. But she did nothing of the kind. She looked down demurely on the deck, with the faint flicker of a smile hovering about her pretty lips, and now and then flashed a quick glance at the serious face of the young man. The attitude was very sweet and appealing, but it was not what we have a right to expect from one whose ruler is her servant towards one whose ruler is his sovereign. In fact, the conduct of those two young people at this time was utterly inexplicable.

"Why did you pretend to Hodden that you had never heard of him, and make him state that he was a writer of books?" Buel had said.

"I did it for his own good. Do you want me to minister to his insufferable vanity? Hasn't he egotism enough already? I saw in a paper a while ago that his most popular book had sold to the extent of over 100,000 copies in America. I suppose that is something wonderful; but what does it amount to after all? It leaves over fifty millions of people who doubtless have never heard of him. For the time being I merely went with the majority. We always do that in the States."

"Then I suppose you will not tell him you bought his latest book in London, and so you will not have the privilege of bringing it up on-deck and reading it?"

"No. The pleasure of reading that book must be postponed until I reach New York. But my punishment does not end there. Would you believe that authors are so vain that they actually carry with them the books they have written?"

"You astonish me."

"I thought I should. And added to that, would you credit the statement that they offer to lend their works to inoffensive people who may not be interested in them and who have not the courage to refuse? Why do you look so confused, Mr. Buel? I am speaking of Mr. Hodden. He kindly offered me his books to read on the way over. He has a prettily bound set with him. He gave me the first to-day, which I read ever so many years ago."

"I thought you liked his books?"

"For the first time, yes; but I don't care to read them twice."

The conversation was here interrupted by Mr. Hodden himself, who sank into the vacant chair beside Miss Jessop. Buel made as though he would rise and leave them together, but with an almost imperceptible motion of the hand nearest him, Miss Jessop indicated her wish that he should remain, and then thanked him with a rapid glance for understanding. The young man felt a glow of satisfaction at this, and gazed at the blue sea with less discontent than usual in his eyes.

"I have brought you," said the novelist, "another volume."

"Oh, *thank* you," cried Miss Duplicity, with unnecessary emphasis on the middle word.

"It has been considered," continued Mr. Hodden, "by those whose opinions are thought highly of in London, to be perhaps my most successful work. It is, of course, not for me to pass judgment on such an estimate; but for my own part I prefer the story I gave you this morning. An author's choice is rarely that of the public."

"And was this book published in America?"

"I can hardly say it was published. They did me the honour to pirate it in your most charming country. Some friend - or perhaps I should say enemy - sent me a copy. It was a most atrocious production, in a paper cover, filled with mistakes, and adorned with the kind of spelling, which is, alas! prevalent there."

"I believe," said Buel, speaking for the first time, but with his eyes still on the sea, "there is good English authority for much that we term American spelling."

"English authority, indeed!" cried Miss Jessop; "as if we needed English authority for anything. If we can't spell better than your great English authority, Chaucer - well!" Language seemed to fail the young woman.

"Have you read Chaucer?" asked Mr. Hodden, in surprise.

"Certainly not; but I have looked at his poems, and they always remind me of one of those dialect stories in the magazines."

Miss Jessop turned over the pages of the book which had been given her, and as she did so a name caught her attention. She remembered a problem that had troubled her when she read the book before. She cried impulsively - "Oh, Mr. Hodden, there is a question I want to ask you about this book. Was -" Here she checked herself in some confusion.

Buel, who seemed to realise the situation, smiled grimly.

"The way of the transgressor is hard," he whispered in a tone too low for Hodden to hear.

"Isn't it?" cordially agreed the unblushing young woman.

"What did you wish to ask me?" inquired the novelist.

"Was it the American spelling or the American piracy that made you dislike the United States?"

Mr. Hodden raised his eyebrows.

"Oh, I do not dislike the United States. I have many friends there, and see much to admire in the country. But there are some things that do not commend themselves to me, and those I ventured to touch upon lightly on one or two occasions, much to the displeasure of a section of the inhabitants - a small section, I hope."

"Don't you think," ventured Buel, "that a writer should rather touch on what pleases him than on what displeases him, in writing of a foreign country?"

"Possibly, Nations are like individuals; they prefer

flattery to honest criticism."

"But a writer should remember that there is no law of libel to protect a nation."

To this remark Mr. Hodden did not reply.

"And what did you object to most, Mr. Hodden?" asked the girl.

"That is a hard question to answer. I think, however, that one of the most deplorable features of American life is the unbridled license of the Press. The reporters make existence a burden; they print the most unjustifiable things in their so-called interviews, and a man has no redress. There is no escaping them. If a man is at all well known, they attack him before he has a chance to leave the ship. If you refuse to say anything, they will write a purely imaginative interview. The last time I visited America, five of them came out to interview me - they came out in the Custom House steamer, I believe."

"Why, I should feel flattered if they took all that trouble over me, Mr. Hodden."

"All I ask of them is to leave me alone."

"I'll protect you, Mr. Hodden. When they come, you stand near me, and I'll beat them off with my sunshade. I know two newspaper men - real nice young men they are too - and they always do what I tell them."

"I can quite believe it, Miss Jessop."

"Well, then, have no fear while I'm on board."

Mr. Hodden shook his head. He knew how it would be, he said.

"Let us leave the reporters. What else do you object to? I want to learn, and so reform my country when I get back."

"The mad passion of the people after wealth, and the unscrupulousness of their methods of obtaining it, seem to me unpleasant phases of life over there."

"So they are. And what you say makes me sigh for dear old London. How honest they are, and how little they care for money there! *They* don't put up the price 50 per cent. merely because a girl has an American accent. Oh no. They think she likes to buy at New York prices. And they are so honourable down in the city that nobody ever gets cheated. Why, you could put a purse up on a pole in London, just as - as - was it Henry the Eighth -?"

"Alfred, I think!" suggested Buel.

"Thanks! As Alfred the Great used to do."

Mr. Hodden looked askance at the young woman.

"Remember," he said, "that you asked me for my opinion. If what I have said is offensive to one who is wealthy, as doubtless you are, Miss Jessop, I most sincerely -"

"Me? Well, I never know whether I'm wealthy or not. I expect that before long I shall have to take to typewriting. Perhaps, in that case, you will give me some of your novels to do, Mr. Hodden. You see, my father is on the Street."

"Dear me!" said Mr. Hodden, "I am sorry to hear that."

"Why? They are not all rogues on Wall Street, in spite of what the papers say. Remember your own opinion of the papers. They are not to be trusted when they speak of Wall Street men. When my father got very rich once I made him give me 100,000 dollars, so that, should things go wrong - they generally go wrong for somebody on Wall Street - we would have something to live on, but, unfortunately, he always borrows it again. Some day, I'm afraid, it will go, and then will come the typewriter. That's why I took my aunt with me and saw Europe before it was too late. I gave him a power of attorney before I left, so I've had an anxious time on the Continent. My money was all right when we left Liverpool, but goodness knows where it will be when I reach New York."

"How very interesting. I never heard of a situation just like it before."

CHAPTER VI.

The big vessel lay at rest in New York Bay waiting for the boat of the health officers and the steamer with the customs men on board. The passengers were in a state of excitement at the thought of being so near home. The captain, who was now in excellent humour, walked the deck and chatted affably with every one. A successful voyage had been completed. Miss Jessop feared the coming of the customs boat as much as Hodden feared the reporters. If anything, he was the more resigned of the two. What American woman ever lands on her native shore without trembling before the revenue laws of her country? Kenan Buel, his arms resting on the bulwarks, gazed absently at the green hills he was seeing for the first time, but his thoughts were not upon them. The young man was in a quandary. Should he venture, or should he not, that was the question. Admitting, for the sake of argument, that she cared for him, what had he to offer? Merely himself, and the debt still unpaid on his first book. The situation was the more embarrassing because of a remark she had made about Englishmen marrying for money. He had resented that on general principles when he heard it, but now it had a personal application that seemed to confront him whichever way he turned. Besides, wasn't it all rather sudden, from an insular point of view? Of course they did things with great rapidity in America, so perhaps she would not object to the suddenness. He had no one to consult, and he felt the lack of advice. He did not want to make a mistake, neither did he wish to be laughed at. Still, the laughing would not matter if everything turned out right. Anyhow, Miss Jessop's laugh was very kindly. He remembered that if he were in any other difficulty he would turn quite naturally to her for advice, although he had known her so short a time, and he regretted that in his present predicament he was debarred from putting the case before her. And yet, why not? He might put the supposititious case of a friend, and ask what the friend ought to do. He dismissed this a moment later. It was too much like what people did in a novel, and besides, he could not carry it through. She would see through the sham at once. At this point he realised that he was just where he began.

"Dear me, Mr. Buel, how serious you look. I am afraid you don't approve of America. Are you sorry the voyage is ended?"

"Yes, I am," answered Buel, earnestly. "I feel as if I had to begin life over again."

"And are you afraid?"

"A little."

"I am disappointed in you. I thought you were not afraid of anything."

"You were disappointed in me the first day, you remember."

"So I was. I had forgotten."

"Will your father come on board to meet you?"

"It depends altogether on the state of the market. If things are dull, he will very likely meet me out here. If the Street is brisk, I won't see him till he arrives home to-night. If medium, he will be on the wharf when we get in."

"And when you meet him I suppose you will know whether you are rich or poor?"

"Oh, certainly. It will be the second thing I ask him."

"When you know, I want you to tell me. Will you?"

"Are you interested in knowing?"

"Very much so."

"Then I hope I shall be rich."

Mr. Buel did not answer. He stared gloomily down at the water lapping the iron side of the motionless steamer. The frown on his brow was deep. Miss Jessop looked at him for a moment out of the corners of her eyes. Then she said, impulsively -

"I know that was mean. I apologise. I told you I did not like to apologise, so you may know how sorry I am. And, now that I have begun, I also apologise for all the flippant things I have said during the voyage, and for my frightful mendacity to poor Mr. Hodden, who sits there so patiently and picturesquely waiting for the terrible reporters. Won't you forgive me?"

Buel was not a ready man, and he hesitated just the

smallest fraction of a second too long.

"I won't ask you twice, you know," said Miss Jessop, drawing herself up with dignity.

"Don't - don't go!" cried the young man, with sudden energy, catching her hand. "I'm an unmannerly boor. But I'll risk everything and tell you the trouble. I don't care a - I don't care whether you are rich or poor. I -"

Miss Jessop drew away her hand.

"Oh, there's the boat, Mr. Buel, and there's my papa on the upper deck."

She waved her handkerchief in the air in answer to one that was fluttering on the little steamer. Buel saw the boat cutting a rapid semicircle in the bay as she rounded to, leaving in her wake a long, curving track of foam. She looked ridiculously small compared with the great ship she was approaching, and her deck seemed crowded.

"And there are the reporters!" she cried; "ever so many of them. I guess Mr. Hodden will be sorry he did not accept my offer of protection. I know that young man who is waving his hand. He was on the *Herald* when I left; but no one can say what paper he's writing for now."

As the boat came nearer a voice shouted -

"All well, Carrie?"

The girl nodded. Her eyes and her heart were too full for speech. Buel frowned at the approaching boat, and cursed its inopportune arrival. He was astonished to hear some one shout from her deck -

"Hello, Buel!"

"Why, there's some one who knows you!" said the girl, looking at him.

Buel saw a man wave his hand, and automatically he waved in return. After a moment he realised that it was Brant the publisher. The customs officers were first on board, for it is ordained by the law that no foot is to tread the deck before theirs; but the reporters made a good second.

Miss Jessop rushed to the gangway, leaving Buel alone. "Hello, Cap!" cried one of the young men of the Press, with that lack of respect for the dignitaries of this earth which is characteristic of them. "Had a good voyage?"

"Splendid," answered the captain, with a smile.

"Where's your celebrity? Trot him out."

"I believe Mr. Hodden is aft somewhere."

"Oh, - Hodden!" cried the young man, profanely; "he's a chestnut. Where's Kenan Buel?"

The reporter did not wait for a reply, for he saw by the crowd around a very flushed young man that the victim had been found and cornered.

"Really, gentlemen," said the embarrassed Englishman, "you have made a mistake. It is Mr. Hodden you want to see. I will take you to him."

"Hodden's played," said one of the young men in an explanatory way, although Buel did not understand the meaning of the phrase. "He's petered out;" which addition did not make it any plainer. "You're the man for our money every time."

"Break away there, break away!" cried the belated Brant, forcing his way through them and taking Buel by the hand. "There's no rush, you know, boys. Just let me have a minute's talk with Mr. Buel. It will be all right. I have just set up the champagne down in the saloon. It's my treat, you know. There's tables down there, and we can do things comfortably. I'll guarantee to produce Buel inside of five minutes."

Brant linked arms with the young man, and they walked together down the deck.

"Do you know what this means, Buel?" he said, waving his hand towards the retreating newspaper men.

"I suppose it means that you have got them to interview me for business purposes. I can think of no other reason."

"I've had nothing to do with it. That shows just how little you know about the American Press. Why, all the money I've got wouldn't bring those men out here to interview anybody who wasn't worth interviewing. It means fame; it means wealth; it means that you have turned the corner; it means you have the world before you; it means everything. Those young men are not reporters to you; they are the heralds of fame, my boy."

A few of them may get there themselves some day, but it means that you have got there *now*. Do you realise that?"

"Hardly. I suppose, then, the book has been a success?"

"A success? It's been a cyclone. I've been fighting pirates ever since it came out. You see, I took the precaution to write some things in the book myself."

Buel looked alarmed.

"And then I copyrighted the whole thing, and they can't tell which is mine and which is yours until they get a hold of the English edition. That's why I did not wait for your corrections."

"We are collaborators, then?"

"You bet. I suppose some of the English copies are on this steamer? I'm going to try to have them seized by the customs if I can. I think I'll make a charge of indecency against the book."

"Good heavens!" cried Buel, aghast. "There is nothing of that in it."

"I am afraid not," said Brant, regretfully. "But it will give us a week more at least before it is decided. Anyhow, I'm ready for the pirates, even if they do come out. I've printed a cheap paper edition, 100,000 copies, and they are now in the hands of all the news companies - sealed up, of course - from New York to San Francisco. The moment a pirate shows his head, I'll telegraph the word 'rip' all over the United States, and they will rip open the packages and flood the market with authorised cheap editions before the pirates leave New York. Oh, L. F. Brant was not born the day before yesterday."

"I see he wasn't," said Buel, smiling.

"Now you come down and be introduced to the newspaper boys. You'll find them jolly nice fellows."

"In a moment. You go down and open the champagne. I'll follow you. I - I want to say a few words to a friend on board."

"No tricks now, Buel. You're not going to try to dodge them?"

"I'm a man of my word, Mr. Brant. Don't be afraid."

"And now," said the other, putting his hands on the young man's shoulders, "you'll be kind to them. Don't put on too much side, you know. You'll forgive me for mentioning this, but sometimes your countrymen do the high and mighty act a little too much. It doesn't pay."

"I'll do my best. But I haven't the slightest idea what to say. In fact, I've nothing to say."

"Oh, that's all right. Don't you worry. Just have a talk with them, that's all they want. You'll be paralysed when the interviews come out to-morrow; but you'll get over that."

"You're sure the book is a success in its own merits, and not through any newspaper puffing or that sort of thing, you know?"

"Why, certainly. Of course our firm pushed it. We're not the people to go to sleep over a thing. It might not have done quite so well with any other house; but I told you in London I thought it was bound to go. The pushing was quite legitimate."

"In that case I shall be down to see the reporters in a very few minutes." Although Buel kept up his end of the conversation with Brant, his mind was not on it. Miss Jessop and her father were walking near them; snatches of their talk came to him, and his attention wandered in spite of himself. The Wall Street man seemed to be trying to reassure his daughter, and impart to her some of the enthusiasm he himself felt. He patted her affectionately on the shoulder now and then, and she walked with springy step very close to his side.

"It's all right, Carrie," he said, "and as safe as the bank."

"Which bank, papa?"

Mr. Jessop laughed.

"The Chemical Bank, if you like; or, as you are just over from the other side, perhaps I should say the Bank of England."

"And did you take put every cent?"

"Yes; and I wished there was double the amount to take. It's a sure thing. There's no speculation about it. There isn't a bushel of wheat in the country that isn't in the combination. It would have been sinful not to have put every cent I could scrape together into it. Why,

Carrie, I'll give you a quarter of a million when the deal comes off."

Carrie shook her head.

"I've been afraid of wheat corners," she said, "ever since I was a baby. Still, I've no right to say anything. It's all your money, anyway, and I've just been playing that it was mine. But I do wish you had left a hundred dollars for a typewriter."

Mr. Jessop laughed again in a very hearty and confident way.

"Don't you fret about that, Carrie. I've got four type machines down at the office. I'll let you have your choice before the crash comes. Now I'll go down and see those customs men. There won't be any trouble. I know them."

It was when Mr. Jessop departed that Buel suddenly became anxious to get rid of Brant. When he had succeeded, he walked over to where the girl leaned on the bulwark.

"Well?" he said, taking his place beside her.

"Well!" she answered, without looking up at him.

"Which is it? Rich or poor?"

"Rich, I should say, by the way the reporters flocked about you. That means, I suppose, that your book has been a great success, and that you are going to make your fortune out of it. Let me congratulate you, Mr. Buel."

"Wait a minute. I don't know yet whether I am to be congratulated or not; that will depend on you. Of course you know I was not speaking of myself when I asked the question."

"Oh, you meant me, did you? Well, I can't tell for some time to come, but I have my fears. I hear the click of the typewriter in the near future."

"Caroline, I am very serious about this. I don't believe you think, or could think, that I care much about riches. I have been on too intimate terms with poverty to be afraid of it. Of course my present apparent success has given me courage, and I intend to use that courage while it lasts. I have been rather afraid of your ridicule, but I think, whether you were rich or poor, or whether my book was a success or a failure, I would have risked it, and told you I loved you."

The girl did not look up at him, and did not answer for a moment. Then she said, in a voice that he had to bend very close to hear -

"I - I would have been sorry all my life if you hadn't - risked it."